Holiday in *Heaven*

Aron Abrahamsen

Holiday in *Heaven*

Introduction by
Dorothy K. Ives

Aron & Doris Abrahamsen
St. Augustine, Florida

Copyright © 1994, 1995, 1998 by Aron Abrahamsen

First Edition
2nd Printing
Printed and bound in the United States of America

All rights reserved. No Part of this book may be reproduced or transmitted in any form or by any means, electronic or mechanical, including photocopying, recording or by any information storage and retrieval system, without permission in writing from the Publisher.

For information contact:
Aron & Doris Abrahamsen
P.O.Box 840008
St. Augustine Beach, FL 32084-0008
Fax: (904) 471-1201
E mail: aandd@aug.com
Web site: http://www.oldcity.com/abrahamsen/

ISBN: 0-9662045-0-6

Library of Congress Catalogue Number: 97-94880

Publications by Aron & Doris Abrahamsen:

Holiday in Heaven

On Wings of Spirit

The New Earth

Attunement of Body, Mind & Spirit through Music and Color

Living in Community

The Abrahamsen Report

Dedicated to my sister and brother Asne and Jacob, who showed me glimpses of life on the other side; and to my beloved wife Doris, who showed me life on this side.

Acknowledgments

I want to thank all the wonderful people who have been of such help in the writing of this book. Their encouragements and positive attitudes during this process have been invaluable to me. In particular I wish to thank my wonderful critique, my beloved wife Doris. Without her help and assistance this book wouldn't be what it is today. I also wish to thank those who took from their valuable time to read the manuscript and give their suggestions--Dorothy Ives, and thanks to her also for writing the introduction; Gillian Spencer; Al Miner; and Diane Lumsden. Thanks also to a wonderful and understanding editor and proof reader, Luana Ewing.

TABLE OF CONTENTS

Foreword	Aron Abrahamsen	
Introduction	Dorothy Ives	
Chapter 1	Visitors from Beyond	1
Chapter 2	Prelude for the Journey	18
Chapter 3	A Sparkling New World	38
Chapter 4	The Akashic Records	57
Chapter 5	Look Who's Coming to Heaven	78
Chapter 6	Heavenly Discussions	92
Chapter 7	Precarious Truth	110
Chapter 8	The Angelic Kingdom	131
Chapter 9	Time and Thought Travel	148
Chapter 10	Visit to Another Universe	158
Chapter 11	Karma Are Us	169
Chapter 12	Think Right -- Live Right	190
Chapter 13	Life Recycling	211
Chapter 14	Journey's End	219

Foreword

Many readers will find much of this information controversial. Yet, if you're open enough to be reading a book authored by me, you're at least willing to explore concepts of truth that go beyond the mainstream and fundamental churches. This is what you'll find here.

The concept for this book came from a dream. Some of the experiences actually happened to me personally, another part is information that I obtained in the altered state. Yet, for all practical purposes I consider this work fiction, set against a background of truth.

The names given in this book, of my sister and brothers, plus other members of my family, including our friend Sonja, were their actual names, as were the names of all of the historical people. Some of the names, which I'm sure that you, the reader, will easily recognize, are purely fictitious. I've given these individuals ridiculous sounding names in an effort to bring in some humor. Those souls chose to remain anonymous.

We all recognize that time as we know it here on the Earth plane does not exist on the other side. As you read this book, please bear with me as I attempt to use time in explaining some of the events.

I invite you to come journey with me for a Holiday in Heaven. I hope that you will enjoy this book as much as I enjoyed writing it.

Aron Abrahamsen

St. Augustine, Florida 1998

Introduction

How sweet indeed is the mystery of life. It has been written about, dramatized, and even sung about. Remember the song, "Ah Sweet Mystery of Life at last I've found thee"? The sweetness of the finding, embracing and unfolding. The mystery lies in the human mind and heart energetically seeking, finding and then sharing the splendor of a blossoming consciousness.

Two such open minded insightful persons entered the magical door of friendship during the last years of my husband Burl Ives earthly sojourn. He was experiencing even then the body's readying itself for the journey home. We knew Doris and Aron Abrahamsen through their book, *On Wings of Spirit*, and the platform of shared ideals. Indeed, 'on wings of spirit' they entered in, sweetly filling our hearts with song and laughter. And so another foundation was formed and we four became as one.

We knew Aron was writing another book, and Burl wanted to pleasure himself by writing an introduction to Aron's most recent work. Since the book was not completed in time for 'My Old Bard' to fulfill his desire, I take pen in hand 'On The Wings of Burl's Spirit,' and with the inspiration I gained as his partner in Oneness, I lovingly invite you, Dear Reader, to journey with Aron into the world now inhabited by Burl. That eternal place of wonder, where more learning and magic so sweetly embrace the splendor of an unfolding mystery.

"Holiday in Heaven" by Aron Abrahamsen, with helpful suggestions from Doris, his partner in Oneness. The book is an embrace. Read, ponder and enjoy. Humor, realization and a timeless place are awaiting your visit.

Yours in Light

Dorothy K. Ives
Anacortes, Washington, 1997

Chapter 1

Visitors from Beyond

I had expected something like this to happen. Yet when it did I was still utterly amazed.
I heard them! I saw them! I touched them!
"Aron, we've come to take you to Heaven!"
"But I'm not dead! I haven't even been sick! I feel fine!"
"We know you aren't dead. But haven't you been wondering what life is like in Heaven? Well, we've come to give you a personal tour."
With that, two large columns of shimmering white light appeared. They seemed to be standing still. And then they started to vibrate - first at a very rapid rate then slower and slower until the white columns of light disappeared. Two figures began to take shape. As they did I recognized them immediately!
"Are you really Asne and Jacob, or am I seeing things?" I questioned. The pit of my stomach was tingling. They were my long departed brother and sister! Needless to say I was more than thrilled.

"Don't get excited, it's really us." Asne replied in a calming voice. (pronounced Ahsne)

Jacob spoke up then. "You have no idea how enormous Heaven is. As you know, Aron, what you have seen in your thousands of journeys to the Akashic records is only like a drop of water in an enormously large ocean. But there is so much more to Heaven. Classes to attend, workshops to learn from, souls to meet and talk with. You'll be surprised to see who is there. The 25 years of journeying to the Records couldn't give you even a glimpse of what's there. We want to satisfy your curiosity about these parts of Heaven.

"If you're willing to come with us," Asne went on, "we can give you a tour of some of the delights in our area of Heaven. We have experienced such beauty and love there! In so many ways we are reminded that we are, and have always been, loved. It's always there for us, and that same love is available to all people on Earth if they will just open up to it. We'd like for you to experience some of this, too! Will you come with us?"

"You bet!" I responded quickly. "I'll get Doris. She's farther down on the beach." I pointed her out to them.

Asne and Jacob placed staying hands on my shoulders. "Sorry," Asne cautioned.

Jacob picked up quickly. "Taking one person on a heavenly tour will tax our abilities as it is. I don't think we could handle two people."

"Besides," Asne was looking toward Doris," she'll hardly know you're gone. Look, your friends

Connie and Jay have joined her. We'll be back real soon."

Reluctantly I agreed. For over 47 years, when at all possible, Doris and I had always done things together. It just didn't seem right to go off without her. I tried to wave to her, but she was searching for colorful stones on the beach and Connie and Jay were looking with her. Maybe I'll be back before she misses me. I could only hope that Jacob and Asne were right.

These thoughts flashed through my mind as we made our way over the white washed logs that long ago had been tossed up on the beach by stormy seas. An occasional call of a seagull, and the gentle lap of the waves accompanied us as we climbed the concrete stairway leading to the road above us.

I stopped a moment to look back over the beach where Doris was.

I remembered that for several days I had been absorbed in thinking about my brother and sister, Jacob and Asne. It was such a long time since I had seen them. What were they doing now? I wondered. They had passed away many years ago. What was it like over there? All this had occupied my thoughts for a long time.

But there was more to my meeting with these two, much more! It concerned an issue that to me was very important, and one for which I had been seeking an answer.

Like a persistent itch a certain thought had invaded my privacy with constant repetition. Sounding like a broken record, it kept asking the same question.

Though I had all the pat answers, that didn't exactly satisfy me.

My memory kept taking me back to 1940, when, as a teenager I first came to America from Norway all by myself. Nobody was there on the dock to meet me when the ship arrived in New York City. I was 18 years old, it was my first time away from home, on my own, and I was terrified! The same experience was repeated later when I returned to Miami, after having obtained my immigration visa in Havana, Cuba. And again when I first arrived in California; again when, as a Navy recruit, I left for boot camp from Los Angeles by train; also when I was discharged from the U.S Navy; as well as when I arrived in San Luis Obispo, California, to start College. Then, on national holidays when most of the students could return home, I had nowhere to go.

I had experienced such a deep loneliness during those times that I didn't want to go through these solitary moments again if I could ever help it. All this made me question whether there would be anyone to meet me on the other side when it was my time to die. Would this solitude continue to follow me even into life after death? Was this a karma that would endlessly hound me?

To me, death would be like arriving in a foreign country--still alone--no one on the dock to meet me.

Since I married Doris in 1950, I have never been lonely again. She has always been there for me. Over a period of many years I have often talked to Doris about this, and she would always reassure me that Asne and Jacob, at least, would be there to meet me. Yet those earlier lonely experiences had left such an imprint on me that I couldn't shake that dread.

At one time I confided in a close friend, Al Miner, about this problem. Al gave me several tapes dealing with this subject. They had been comforting, yet, I suppose that my psyche was overwhelmed by all that loneliness before Doris came into my life. I was still afraid that if we were separated by death those lonely events--even in Heaven--would face me again.

On the day of this extraordinary visit from my brother and sister, I was in my 70's and in good health. I wondered if I would live as long as my mother who had died at 96. A number of my family members-- including my parents, most of my relatives and many college class mates had passed away by now. I wondered what life was like for them on the other side.

Then I remembered a dream I had in which Asne appeared to me. It had happened several years ago when Doris and I were fulfilling a speaking engagement in Florida. The details of that dream and the meditation that followed had etched themselves into my memory bank. At the time, the message from that dream was reassuring. Nevertheless, now I needed to know if that understanding was still valid. I was wishing I could talk to Asne. It would be such a unique experience to visit the other side, even if only for a short time, like a day. But of course, such an adventure would be impossible.

Sitting at the beach that day, I may have appeared to others to be a lonely man, but I wasn't. Yes, I was alone, but never lonely any more. I had Doris, and I had made friends with myself, with nature and with God; and had for a long time enjoyed the anticipation of discovering something new every day. For many weeks Doris and I had been coming to this little beach area. I had a permanent reservation for the same log to sit on. There I was, absorbed in wondering whether such an adventure might be conceivable. This must be why Asne and Jacob have appeared to me, I reasoned to myself.

"Jacob and I are going to try to make it possible for you to see what life is like on the other side," Asne was saying.

My heart began to beat rapidly as I gasped "I can hardly wait!"

"We want to help you find some answers to your questions." Jacob added.

"I welcome any help you can give!" I exclaimed. "In fact, I have a question for you now. That was a spectacular entrance you two made, with all the brilliant light. How did you do that?"

"It's an intricate and complex process" Jacob obliged. "On the other side we vibrate at a much higher frequency than most of you on Earth. The higher the vibration the brighter and more intense is the light. We all vibrate at different frequencies depending upon our consciousness. Yet to the untrained consciousness, we all look the same.

"After we arrive on the other side, and when we are ready to learn, we're trained to lower our vibration anytime we wish to visit Earth in a physically manifested form. Of course, we also learn to raise our vibration to its former level so that we may return to Heaven when our visit is over. When you first saw us here we were still in a high vibratory state, and had only started to lower our vibratory level to the point where we could manifest in the flesh as you see us now.

"When we leave here," Jacob continued, "Asne and I reverse the process and turn our physical body into light. Our conscious minds raise our own vibrations. As we continue to raise our vibrations our light shifts from visible to invisible, and we disappear from your sight. From then on we are free to journey to our next destination. That's how it is done. If you want to know all the details, it may be explained to you later."

"That is very interesting," I exclaimed. "I hope we'll be able to discuss it later."

For some unexplained reason I was reminded of a visit with Asne in 1958. It was such a long time ago, more than 30 years, since I had last seen her. Doris and I had been on a vacation to Amsterdam, where my other sister, Beile, lived. Asne had arrived from Stockholm, to be with us. Both of them were waiting at Schipol Airport when we arrived. Beile had arranged for us to stay at a bed & breakfast place. Asne was staying in the room next to ours, and we were looking forward to spending some time with her. I remembered the profound conversations we had with Asne about our spiritual experiences, and the changes that had taken place within herself as well as those in myself since we were last together in 1940.

"You don't look very happy." I observed out loud during one of our many conversations. "No, I'm not." She admitted honestly. Her deep brown eyes looked away reflecting her longing for the secure and stable time she once had. "My best friend, (you remember Sonja) committed suicide not long ago. Without her I feel lost. She was my constant confidant."

"Is there something you'd like to confide in us" I asked quietly.

"A few years ago," she sighed deeply, "I entered the hospital for an operation--a very serious one--the doctor told me. I was terrified. You remember, Aron, I lost a lung before the war, and that left me in a weakened condition. The doctor couldn't assure me that I'd pull through this one. I was so concerned for my little girls. Who would care for them if I didn't make it?

"Then, the night before the operation I couldn't sleep. Around midnight, I suppose, a bright column of light appeared in the far right corner of my hospital room. I was too scared at first to speak, and too tired to think. The light came next to my bed and told me not to worry, that I'd live through the operation. All my apprehension melted away as I was surrounded with an incredible love.

"Afterwards I didn't dare to share that experience with anyone except Sonja and Jacob. Do you think it might have been an angel?" I assured her it was.

We both spoke freely about our spiritual awakenings, and by the end of the day it appeared that both of us had gone through similar spiritual experiences at about the same time. A special bond developed between the three of us. (Shortly after our return home Asne passed away.)

After our visit to Amsterdam, we traveled to Norway, and my home town Trondheim, where we had many absorbing and penetrating talks with Jacob.

Asne interrupted my thoughts. "We wanted so much to see you that we consulted with our guides about it. Do you know about guides?"

She didn't wait for my answer.

"A guide is a soul who through diligent and dedicated service has been elevated to the position of helping others with advice and counsel.

"So we told our guides all about you, and how you had a number of persistent questions on your mind. They encouraged us to try to help you!

" Now," Asne declared triumphantly, "if you're willing, we hope to show you a portion of Heaven, and something of what life is like on the other side."

"That's wonderful!" I exclaimed. As I looked at them I marveled at how young and healthy they appeared. Here was Jacob, dressed in a three piece light beige striped suit, a sharp crease down his pants, front and back, brightly polished brown shoes, light beige socks, a matching striped tie was elegantly tied over a crisp white shirt, with French cuffs held together by gold cuff links showing under his coat sleeves. A light beige summer hat was cocked to the right, and as always, his right hand was attached to an umbrella. He could have easily stepped right out of a showroom.

My mind instantly shot back to Norway where we all grew up, and I remembered how fastidious and fashionable he had always been. For him to be dressed otherwise would have been unthinkable.

I remembered how Jacob, prior to his death, had been a quiet and thoughtful person. He was a deep thinker, being very serious much of the time. His dental practice was considered one of the finest in Norway, and his office was used as a model for the students from the dental college in Oslo. In addition he was a pianist, a composer, and a champion bridge and chess player.

He was also a man of decision. When he made up his mind to take action he did it without consulting anybody, neither family nor friends. At one time Jacob and his brother Julius were practicing dentistry in the same small town where we lived. Both advertising themselves as Dr. J. Abrahamsen, Dentist. However, that became confusing to their patients, who invariably got mixed up and went to the wrong dentist. Jacob got Julius' patients and vice versa. After a few months with that seemingly endless problem Jacob took action. Through the court system he legally changed his name to Ilevik. The confusion among their patients vanished.

It hadn't always been easy for him. When he first opened his dental practice in Oslo, it was a real struggle. I'm sure he missed many meals--not because he was on a diet. Patients were as few as snowflakes in Florida. He was behind in his rent, yet never asked the family for help. He wanted to make it on his own. Through friends of Jacob, my older brother Heiman, learned of his desperate plight. He took the train from Trondheim to Oslo, helped Jacob close his office, paid the back rent, and took him back to Trondheim. There, a suitable location for his dental practice was found.

Though Jacob was decisive in most matters, there was an inconsistency when it came to his personal love life. There his extremely shy nature prevailed.

For years he had secretly been in love with Sonja, a beautiful, musically talented young Jewish girl. She was also in love with him, but neither had the resolve to make their feelings known to each other. At one time, Oskar, another of my eight brothers, encouraged him to ask Sonja to marry him. Yet Jacob could never muster the courage to follow through, even after Oskar had assured him that Sonja was also in love with him. None of us could understand why he held back.

"Do you still play bridge and chess?" I asked, wondering if Jacob had perhaps found some other hobbies--like gardening or writing.

"Yes, I still play bridge and chess--only better. There are some clever teachers on the other side. I'm learning a lot. I don't like gardening or writing." He had picked up on my thoughts.

"Are you doing anything in particular to prepare yourself for another incarnation?"

"For one thing, I've decided not to continue in dentistry when I return. I was never really happy in it. It wasn't my idea to become a dentist. It was Mamma's. I wanted to be a composer. But no! I was told I couldn't make a living as a musician. Mama won out. Of course, I knew she had my best interests in mind.

"My happiest moments were at the piano. Right now I'm learning highly advanced composition. There's a lot to it. With this I may be able to prepare myself for another career, like music therapy, in my next life. The teaching on the other side is that music and color therapy, and other related disciplines, will be the main healing methods on planet Earth in the near future. I want to be in on it. This is exciting to me!

"I'm also learning to have the determination of my convictions so that I won't fall into the same trap that I did before."

This I didn't know about Jacob. I had always believed that being a dentist made him as happy as a clam at high tide.

"One more thing," Jacob added, "I don't think I'll be returning to Norway in my next life. Australia looks more appealing to me."

"Why not the United States?" I inquired.

"Too many problems. Big ones. Real big ones. It'll probably get worse. Doesn't seem that anyone wants to solve them. All I can hear is talk, talk, talk. No leadership. That country isn't what it used to be. No thanks. I think Australia, or someplace around there, has the best chance of taking the lead, if the United States doesn't regain her status. Maybe even China, provided it isn't under a polar ice cap and has become the north pole. I'm at least considering these countries unless there is service for me elsewhere. I'll make that decision later anyway."

"You want to hear what I'm preparing for?" Asne broke in.

"Of course!" I responded.

"Well," she cleared her throat, "I am determined not to repeat my past mistakes. I have felt like a cork in the ocean of life for too long."

She is right, I thought. She had wanted a career in music and the theater, but it was forbidden by our parents. So she just drifted around.

"I'm spending lots of time working on goals, motives and intentions before I reincarnate." She emphasized "before" by squinting. "I attend classes all the time for learning the basics, like being honest with myself, loyal to my highest intentions, coupled with discernment and patience. It isn't easy for me, nevertheless I know I'll make a better life for myself next time around.

"I'm also taking classes in music and drama. That's the field I want to be in so that I can contribute something of beauty to the world. I'm tired of wandering around. I've done that for too long."

Her face lit up like a display of fireworks, her eyes became big and determined. "I'll do it, too. Just wait and see!"

Her determination was obvious, and I was sure she would accomplish much in her next life time.

"By the way," I was curious, "how did the two of you find me here? How did you know that I was living in this area and not in California or Oregon?"

"Where we come from," Asne explained, "there is a complete register of everybody's whereabouts. The central filing system is really something to behold. The method you people on Earth use to maintain large data banks is so outmoded it is akin to the stone age."

"But how did you know that I was on the beach?"

"We asked at Old Salts, your local deli. They knew where you were. We also stopped over at the Beach Club and talked to Peggy. She told us you'd probably be on the beach. Is everyone in this area so friendly? We also met John Waters. He was such a helpful man. Even offered to take us to where you were. He knew that we had no transportation. Declining his offer, we thanked him, and headed on over here by thought travel."

"Thought travel!" I blurted out. "How are you able to do that?"

"Thought travel," Asne obliged, "is achieved when the mind is able to raise the vibrations of the physical body so that the thought destination and the body become as one. Wherever the thoughts journey the body will follow. You might hear more about it when you get to the other side with us. By the way, when we travel on Earth we change our body into light, when we journey outside the solar system we use thought travel. As you saw earlier we used light travel to find you. Of course, we waited to use that form of travel until we were out of the presence of your friends. We didn't want to startle them."

I had to remind myself that so much had happened in just a few minutes. Right in front of me were two members of my family who had been dead for many years and now had materialized right before my eyes, and we were actually talking with each other!

"Don't stare at us as if we are from a circus." Asne declared.

"We are perfectly normal," Jacob added, "in case you didn't notice. We breathe the air. We can touch and feel like you do. We also get hungry. But there is another thing we can do, besides thought and light travel, that you can't, at least for now. We can read your mind like an open book. I know that some on the Earth plane do this, but right now it isn't one of your skills. We can read everybody's mind. For the most part it's pretty dull reading."

We walked in silence for a moment, absorbing the fresh air and clear sunshine. There was so much I wanted to ask them. Especially, whether there would be anyone to meet me when I crossed over. I wondered how I might properly approach this issue.

I looked at Jacob on my right. Slender and thin haired, about 5 feet 7 inches with calm contemplating eyes and fair complexion. As usual he was silent, and when he spoke, his words were carefully chosen.

I continued reflecting.

I'm not a very tall man, myself, a few inches shorter than six feet. In my teens I had a full head of curly black hair, but like the passing years, that too is gone. There is now only a thin rim of light gray hair around my head.

Doris tells me that my dark brown eyes express wonderment at just about everything I find to be new and challenging. In my later years I developed a curiosity for many different fields and subjects. This was quite a departure from my younger days. In those years I had time only for my engineering career, studying the Bible, and being very active in our church. I felt so sure of my theology that I took great pains to persuade others to my belief system.

That, however, had changed. Through much soul searching and further study, I began to realize that my obsession with agreement on religious matters had limited my spiritual growth. This had taken some years for me to recognize; and then it became quite clear to me that I didn't have all the truth after all. I had to admit that I was the hard-headed one, and that I was also intolerant. None of these realizations were easy for me to acknowledge.

By now I was no longer interested in convincing others that I had all the truth, for I knew I didn't. People, I had come to believe, had to discover truth for themselves. I couldn't prove anything to them. They had to prove the truth to themselves.

Asne on my left was as beautiful as she had ever been. I admired her black hair and those marvelous brown eyes. In her earlier years she had always been the life of the party, entertaining everybody with her songs, music and humor. Very few people had the privilege of seeing the thoughtful side of her personality.

When we were together in Amsterdam Asne had confided in me that for many years she had wanted to better understand life and all its ramifications. She would often ask herself what she was doing on Earth, what her purpose was and how she could accomplish it. The family and relatives seemed to take no time for serious spiritual thought. The only thing they could think of was humor, laughing at others, and working hard to make a living. "What else is there in life?" she had been told a number of times. So she gave up and went along with the family.

However, when she saw an opportunity to delve into a serious discussion, she always participated, with guarded words, of course. She didn't want to be made fun of by the family.

I thought back to my own childhood, and my desire to read poetry. I had bought a number of poetry books, and read them in secret, always alert, lest the other family members should approach. To prevent anyone from discovering my secret, I hid my books in a place where I hoped nobody would find them. They never did. I didn't dare to talk about poetry to anyone in the family. Like Asne, I didn't want to be made fun of.

I took the same approach after I had seen the movie "A Midsummer Night's Dream." I had come away from the movie theater spellbound, but I never told anyone about how it had affected me. I also felt that I had no one to talk to about these things.

Asne began, "We're trying to find a way to start answering what's on your mind. You have so many concerns we don't know where to begin."

I was grateful and relieved to know that my questions would soon be answered. But there were some issues I wanted answers to before Asne and Jacob addressed themselves to my other concerns.

Chapter 2

Prelude for the Journey

While we continued our walk I asked Jacob why he had waited so long before he went to the hospital? Oskar, one of my eight brothers, had told me by phone that Jacob had suffered chest pains for a number of months. That should have been sufficient warning, I thought, that his life might be in danger.

"I had those pains on and off for several years, and believed it was only indigestion. Nothing serious had ever happened. But then on March 25, 1982, when I got some very severe chest pains, I thought this was the same as had previously occurred. I expected relief to come as usual as it always had before. But this time the pain didn't go away.

"Shortly after noon that day, the pain became worse. I decided to go for a walk, hoping that would relieve the discomfort. I left my office around 2:00 and started to walk very slowly towards the hospital. I arrived there about thirty minutes later. By then the pain had become much worse. I went to the emergency room and asked for something to ease my chest pain.

"The doctor on duty took one look at me and told me to sit down. I protested because I didn't have the time; there were patients waiting in my office. I had to get back as soon as possible. The physician paid no attention to me. He gave me a quick examination, called the orderly and told him to take me to a room and put me to bed. I asked him how long it would take before I could leave. He didn't answer. I guess he knew more than he wanted to tell me.

"Once in bed I felt sick all over, and the pain was excruciatingly intense. I was given massive doses of morphine, which helped a little."

"Did you have any idea that you might be dying?" I asked. "And were you afraid to die?"

For many years I had wanted to know if at the moment of death people had any fear of dying. Jacob and Asne had been through that process and they ought to know. Here was my chance to find an answer.

Jacob gave that question a little time to settle in his thoughts, and after a few moments he answered: "As I was lying in bed feeling all the pain and discomfort, the thought did occur to me that I might leave my body, but I dismissed it. After all, hadn't mother lived to 96 years? I had a long way to go to catch up with her. I believed that longevity was an inherited right, and I wasn't going to leave ahead of my time.

"But the pain kept getting worse, even with all the medication I received. So I wished that if the pain wasn't going to leave that I could leave. As you may remember, I used to analyze a lot. I tried to evaluate the situation as best I could, but because of all the pain it was difficult to gather my thoughts. I was wondering what was going to happen to me.

"All of this took place while I kept my eyes closed so as not to have my thoughts distracted by all the noise and commotion that was taking place around my bed. Then suddenly I knew that every system in my body was starting to shut down: first my kidneys, then the hormone and enzyme systems, one after the other. It was as if I heard 'click, click, click', like relays opening when electrical systems are shutting down. I tried to talk to these parts of my body and urged them to keep on working, especially my heart, but the pain was too great. And I wasn't able to form any coherent thoughts or give definite commands to these various systems.

"I began to be aware of a heavenly chorus and I could see the angelic choir itself. It was so glorious I didn't care about anything else. The music overshadowed any of the pain I had been feeling. If there had been any fear of dying before I experienced this, I wasn't aware of it by this time.

"Suddenly a bright light appeared in my room. As my eyes became more accustomed to it, I could see outlines of three people. Then I saw it was Mama, Asne and Sonja."

"You remember, Aron," Asne broke in, "Sonja was Jacob's dear friend back in the '30s."

"Yes, I remember her well," I replied. "She was very beautiful and talented."

Jacob continued: "Naturally I was surprised to see them and asked what they were doing here. Mama explained that they had come to escort me to the other side. But I told her I wasn't ready to go yet; and when I was, I was sure I could find my own way. They listened and made no comment. They just stayed with me, and I was glad they did.

"At this time I became aware that I was hovering up near the ceiling observing the frantic activity of the nurses and doctors. From what they were saying, I knew that my internal systems had completely shut down.

"Then something very unusual happened. I heard a popping sound, like when a cork is removed from a champagne bottle. To me it sounded so loud I was sure the medical team in the room could hear it. But evidently they didn't, because none of them indicated that they had heard it. The only thing they were aware of was the activity around my bed.

"We're losing him! Quick! Hurry before it's too late!" I clearly heard all the commotion and disturbance as they were working around my body. I knew then that I was dying.

"Suddenly everything became quiet!

"Very quiet!

"Twelve hours after I had entered the hospital I was pronounced dead.

"Instantly I also knew that the popping sound I heard prior to my departure was that of the silver cord being severed. I later learned that the silver cord is the attachment the soul uses to connect itself to the physical body. It isn't a physical cord, of course, but a spiritual one. This attachment is necessary so the soul can find its way back to its body during times of astral projection, or in the case of near-death experiences.

You can say that this cord is something like a bungy cord, and it can stretch itself for many, many miles.

"So the curtain went down for you then," I added.

"You're wrong," Jacob corrected me with a triumphant smile.

"The curtain went up! I was about to encounter a new life.

"It was very fascinating to realize that although my physical body was dead, yet I was still very much alive. This reminded me that my real self was not my physical body, but that my body was the vehicle I used while on the Earth plane.

"I noticed that all the pain was gone, and I felt free and at peace. I tried to explain this to those around my bed, but it was no use; they couldn't hear me. No matter how loud I shouted they paid no attention. At that moment I really believed they were ignoring me on purpose. Mama and Asne told me time and again that the state I was in made it impossible for anyone on the physical plane to hear me. But I didn't believe them and had to find out for myself.

"Then Oskar appeared in the room, and tearfully paid his last respects. I followed him down the hallway as he left, trying to get his attention. Mama and Asne kept telling me, 'He can neither hear you nor see you.' It was very frustrating that nobody paid any attention to me. I would like to have told them that I was still alive.

"What I've learned from many I've met on the other side is that fear at the moment of death is almost nonexistent. Prior to their passing there are visitations from the other side by relatives, friends and angels (similar to my experience). They are such a comforting welcome committee that the person ready to make the transition has no thought of fear. Sometimes a whole choir of angels, with an accompanying orchestra, will make an appearance to a soul who is ready to make the transition.

"Departing from the physical world to the next one is like passing from one room to another. However, it's possible that if the person fights the counsel and comfort given by the welcoming committee, he could very easily develop fear. So you see, it's all up to the individual how to accept the visitations from beyond."

After a short pause Jacob looked at me and asked: "I detect that inasmuch as you have asked this question about fear at the time of death, that you are afraid of death; and if that's the case do you know what is the reason for that?"

"The biggest reason," I responded, "might be because there may not be anyone to meet me when I get to the other side. Remember when I left home before the invasion of Norway? For the next ten years there was never anyone to meet me or to see me off when I traveled. It was a lonely time for me. Now, just the thought of arriving in a strange place by myself brings on those lonely and scary feelings. These experiences always caused me to want to know the exact details of any journey I take, whether I go on vacation or business.

"For my own security and peace of mind I make great efforts to plan as completely as possible to minimize any unexpected surprises. I try to be prepared for every eventuality, but that's not really possible. The thought of going through this aspect of the death experience makes me feel insecure and unwanted. Other than that I'm really just extremely curious about life on your side. What will I find there and what will I be doing are among the many questions running around in my mind. But listening to the explanation of your death process, and how you accepted the transition, helps me understand it better. Please go on; I'm eager to hear the rest."

Asne broke in here: "when your time comes to make the transition, keep in mind that death is not the end; neither is birth the beginning. The terms death and birth are used on the Earth plane to designate the passing of your soul and spirit from one experience to another in the continual cycle of your development. You have been aware of this truth for many years, haven't you?"

"Yes I have, and I appreciate you reminding me of that aspect. I so often forget," I acknowledged. "What happened then after the silver cord was broken?"

"Mama, Asne and Sonja took me through a tunnel. I could see a bright light at the far end," Jacob went on. "When we came into the light, I felt such peace and tranquillity."

"Was that as far as you went?"

"We crossed a river and stepped into a lovely garden. There I met an attendant who checked my name off his list."

"Are you sure that everybody who leaves the physical world meets someone who will take them to where they should be?" I asked.

"Let me tell you how it happened to me," Asne responded. "When I made the transition my good friend Sonja came and escorted me first through the tunnel and then to the Great Library, where I stayed for quite a while. After that I met some other friends and relatives who had gone before me including my grandmother Asne. She died before you were born, Aron. Finally I was assigned to a teacher, and to the classes I was encouraged to take. It was all so easy and wonderful, and I had no fear. All those I met were very helpful. Didn't you find it that way also, Jacob?"

I wanted to ask my sister a number of questions about the Great Library, what she did there, who her teacher was and to what classes she was assigned. With her eyes she directed my attention to Jacob instead.

I was eager to hear all that Jacob and Asne had to tell me. I was so impatient. I wanted the information right now--preferably everything in one sitting. I became fidgety. Was Jacob ever going to say anything more?

He was silent. "That's right." Then silence again. He was in deep thought again, which was his usual behavior. He certainly hadn't changed much over these many years.

Asne and I looked at Jacob, waiting for him to continue his story. He took his time; nobody rushed him. From past experience I knew that if Jacob felt rushed, he would just as well clam up and say nothing, or just as soon walk away. Finally, after a silence that seemed an eternity to me, he looked up, smiled and continued.

"It was all so peaceful and quiet," Jacob continued. "Mama and Sonja excused themselves, saying that Asne would show me around. Together we walked along a path that seemed to consist of clouds. It was wide enough for only the two of us. I asked where she was taking me. 'To The Great Library,' she answered.

"I argued with her that I didn't need to go to any library. I hadn't borrowed any books from it, so nothing was overdue. 'Is that all there is to do here?' I asked her, 'to spend time in the library? I have read so many books in my life, I'd like to do something else. Besides, I don't even have a library card for this library.'

"Asne didn't say a word, just looked at me and kept on walking. After a while she told me that because I was new here I needed somebody to guide me through the introductory steps. 'Much of what you'll see and hear you've seen before, but don't be too concerned if you don't remember it.' She reminded me that there was much for me to learn, and that there was no time for me to waste.

"We continued walking along that path and I was surprised to see that there was no one else on it. I remarked that this must be a private trail.

"She told me that it was an individual approach for those who were on it, and that this passage was not the only one. There are millions of paths to the Great

Library, and those on it are guaranteed strict privacy with their companion.

"It appeared to be a long trail, but we moved along quickly. The pain which I had experienced in the hospital never returned."

"Now I'll hear it all," I thought. I wished I had brought my tape recorder or note paper.

"Forget about the tape recorder and note paper," Jacob interrupted my thought. "You can't write as fast as I talk, and even if you had a tape recorder with you, our voices won't record." Jacob looked at me, "You keep forgetting that Asne and I can read your thoughts."

"Before you go on," I interrupted, "how come you speak such fluent English? Neither of you ever spoke this language that well when you were in your physical bodies."

"I'll explain how it works," Asne remarked. "Within our minds there are certain receptors that store, in a coded format, every language we have ever spoken. When in the physical world it is difficult for most people to access these various languages at will, unless they are linguists and have learned to switch from one language to another.

"But when you leave the physical body, which is a barrier for accessing what is stored in the subconscious mind, you'll have a free approach to whatever is stored there. For the subconscious is part of your spiritual body. Whether it is languages, music, science, or whatever else, you have ready access to it all--provided, of course, that you have learned some of these skills while on Earth.

"Remember," she continued, "that the mind is a more sophisticated computer than any you have seen. What you put in is what you can, with some careful training and a little patience, retrieve--nothing more.

"For example," she continued," if you have learned to paint or compose music in an earlier lifetime, it is quite possible that these skills can be retrieved and used and improved upon in your present life here in the physical plane. However, you should determine your motives for retrieving these latent talents and skills that you had developed earlier.

"While I am on this subject, let me share something that I heard my teacher tell us. In one of his classes we were discussing the subject of talents and genius, and he said that there is no such thing as genius. A genius is any ordinary person who has taken advantage of opportunities, either in one field or a variety of fields presented to it throughout many lifetimes. In each incarnation that soul has worked diligently on these opportunities, with serious and consistent effort to develop in these fields.

"After many incarnations the person finally comes to the place where these skills come more easily. The strong points are developed and expanded in that lifetime in such a way that the soul is considered a genius. Becoming a genius was not the purpose; being the best possible in that field was. The opportunity to give your best is presented to everyone. Some take better advantage of the opportunities than others.

"Take, for example, the soul known on planet Earth as Mozart. In one lifetime in Atlantis he was making musical instruments. After a number of years in that trade he still wasn't very good at it, but he improved, though slowly, over the years. He also took lessons as a boy on an instrument similar to what is now called the piano. But he really wasn't very serious about this until he was an adult. Then he worked furiously to improve his piano skills so as to make up for lost time. In that lifetime he was just an ordinary 'garden variety' person. It was in the subsequent lifetimes that he took music and composition more seriously, and even then he never became famous.

"Not until the 1700s, when he requested to be born into the Mozart family, did all the previous hard work pay off. He was called a genius from his early years, whereas he had committed himself to the field of music through many lifetimes and ---"

"I'm led to believe, from what you're telling me," I interrupted, "that there is really nothing special about a genius. But if that is so, why aren't there more of them? If everybody can be a genius, why aren't they? Are you sure that you remember this right?"

"I'm very sure, because I questioned my teacher about this subject a number of times, and each time the answer was the same: namely, that all you need is the opportunity, the determination and the will-power to persist with what you have started. In other words, never give up. That's what makes them special."

I thought for a moment, then responded with, "That's encouraging! So there is hope for everyone. Now, Asne, you have explained that people can access from their minds any information learned in past lives, like languages, skills, or whatever. However, you're also saying that a person can think and function this way more readily without a physical body while on the non-physical plane."

"Of course," Asne replied, "only much better. The physical body is only a shell (sometimes not a comfortable one at that) that we need in order to communicate and live in a physical world. The physical body has its limitations, and if you overload it--by working too long and hard, or by excessive worry or living an abominable life style--it will soon be worn out, and then it will die. Then you have to leave that body and go to a different plane. However, whether in a physical body or not, you are still alive.

"How can a person learn to retrieve what the mind has stored from a previous physical life?" I wasn't about to stop asking questions.

"It can be learned with diligent discipline, no matter where in the universe you are. The problem has been, and still is, that not too many people are fascinated by such an approach. Most people want instant learning, instant wisdom, instant answers. All are looking for a short-cut. However, the only such short-cut available is discipline, obedience to universal principles, and determination. But don't forget, that which is more important in life is honesty and integrity, and a high moral value system. Understand that retrieving knowledge and skills from the past is not advantageous to the spiritual growth of the soul without these attributes."

"All that you've said confirms much of what I've learned over the past 25 years. Now, Jacob, can you tell me anything more about the events immediately following your passing?" I questioned eagerly."

Jacob responded, "Let me go back a little. You know that many people have left their bodies, hovered over themselves, and observed events taking place. Of course, as you already know, they weren't able to communicate with anyone in the physical world. As you heard me say, I did the same thing; so that isn't anything unusual. However, if their silver cord is still attached when they're having an out-of-body or a near-death experience, they can get back into their bodies quite readily. However, it was different with me!

"As soon as I was out of my body, the silver cord was cut, meaning that I couldn't get back into my body. You remember I said earlier, the silver cord is the psychic cord that connects the soul to the physical body, and is part of the spiritual make-up of the soul. When the connection was broken, that was the sure signal that my body was dead, as you would call it. Any more questions?"

"Oh, yes. I've read about people who have been declared actually dead, yet have come back to life after a while. They report having gone through an experience similar to yours, that they had gone through a tunnel and had come into a place of great peace, just as you had. How does this differ from your experience?"

"There are some similarities as well as some differences " Jacob answered. "Yes they're out of the body. They go through a tunnel; they arrive in a place that is saturated with beauty, peace and love. But in their case, although declared dead, the silver cord is not yet broken and they can't stay at the other end of the tunnel. They have to return to the physical plane, and they're usually told that. If they're given a choice and they decide not to return, then the silver cord is severed to release them."

"Here is another question for you," I persisted. "How is it that some souls after death can return to visit their loved ones or friends, as you are doing? Is there a specific rule that covers these cases?" I was vitally interested in what was taking place on the other side, and how communications were maintained with those of us on planet Earth.

Asne looked thoughtfully at me and started to explain. She closed her eyes for a moment as if she was listening to a silent voice. Her lips became tight, as they used to before she died, when she was concentrating her thoughts.

"You see, a soul can communicate with those on Earth in a number of different ways. The soul can appear in a dream, in a vision, in spirit or in physical form, as Jacob and I are doing now. This sometimes comes as a result of a deep intense cry, on the subconscious level, for help, comfort or assistance in carrying out the daily activities from the one remaining behind. It would be better if the departed soul didn't feel the necessity to return to the loved ones, for that could impede the soul's progress on the other plane.

"Sometimes the appearance may come shortly after crossing to the other side, or it could be in a year. The departed souls are allowed to make the visits in response to the needs they feel must be addressed. Of course, weddings graduations, and such events are always occasions for special visits.

"However, after some time the soul becomes so involved with the affairs on the non-physical plane that it seldom has the time to return to loved ones. It also has its own development and growth to consider, which may make its visits to the physical world less frequent. No matter where a soul is, this responsibility to grow never diminishes. There is always the challenge of growth and maturity on the horizon of the soul. However, while the soul is in the non-physical environment, it also has a responsibility to itself to prepare for another incarnation to planet Earth if that is found to be helpful."

"I'm so sorry that you've had to interrupt your training just because I have some questions," I said.

"No, no," both Asne and Jacob insisted, "it's not a problem," Asne went on. "Besides, we on the other plane know that you will share this information with others and help answer their needs, too. Please now, you have other questions?"

"Well, how does the soul on the other side know that it is needed on the Earth? And how does it know who is calling?" I questioned.

"Although a soul has passed on, it still has feelings, longings and needs. Just because it has laid aside the physical shell, it isn't emotionless, or stoic, and it also experiences a deep sense of loneliness, just as the ones left behind. It has journeyed from a familiar environment to one that, (while unspeakably beautiful and peaceful) for the moment is unknown and strange.

"And although in the new environment, the souls meet relatives, loved ones and friends who passed over earlier, they still miss the ones they have left behind. Habits formed over a lifetime, memories of special events and people on Earth, remain vivid in the files of the subconscious. But the loved ones also have a responsibility to learn and to grow through their experience of loss and grief. Therefore, the departed soul and its guides come to a mutual agreement as to which needs it will respond.

"Being tuned to the particular vibration of a loved one, the call will be answered either in a dream, vision or spirit form, or in a personal appearance with a physical body. There are no limitations as to what form of appearance can be used.

"Nevertheless, the soul is concerned that those left behind need to get on with their lives, and for the benefit of the growth of their loved ones will not respond to every call. Cruel as that may seem, it is best for all."

"Would you say that the departed ones, in visiting Earth, are similar to angels or guardian spirits?"

"There is a similarity here," Asne replied. "These visiting souls can give comfort and hope to their loved ones, friends and former associates. But that's their limit. They have, if you will, a limited service to a limited number of people."

"What do you mean with that?"

"Just as I said. A departed soul can only do so much within the time allotted. It can only visit those whom it has known while on Earth. This is my understanding of visitations by departed souls.

"However, an angel can visit anybody at any given time when the needs are there, to give guidance, direction or re-direction, hope and encouragement. Angels can appear at any time, anywhere to anyone, to assist those who seek help and comfort.

"They can surface as a bright light, an angelic figure dressed in white and with wings--or without wings--in your dreams, in a vision, or as any ordinary person you may see on the street or in your workplace. An angel may never tell you that you're being visited by an angel; that's usually left for you to figure out--which often happens only after the angel has departed.

"The important thing is to be on the alert, for you never know when such a visitation may take place, be it an angel or a departed loved one or friend. I am sure you understand these differences, don't you?"

"Oh yes," I agreed. "You cleared that up for me. I'm glad you know so much about Heaven. So what is life like in Heaven?" I asked.

"Where we are for the present it is called the first heaven," Asne replied. "Life in the first heaven is something like what you experience on Earth. We aren't that far removed from the earthly environment, except we don't have our physical body. Being without it offers us a great deal of freedom. Once you've experienced living without your physical body, living in it would be like being in a prison. But in the first heaven we are experiencing a freedom that is difficult to describe.

"Because we are still very closely connected to our immediate past life on Earth, there still remains the emotions--anger, envy, frustrations, and even hatred-- among many. Those who wanted to get "even" with others, or refused to have any associations with those who have different belief systems, are still in the same frame of mind. They have to begin to change these attitudes before they can move up to the second level.

"You'd be surprised what takes place in the first heaven," Asne continued. "Jacob and I have seen attitudes that could easily lead to demonstrations and long speeches, if they weren't kept so busy with classwork. If they could, one religious group would try to keep out all the other religious groups, thinking that Heaven is only for them. Anything else?"

"Yes, of course. I now have another question for you." I looked at my sister inquisitively while quickly choosing from all my other questions which one to ask. As long as I had the opportunity, I might as well find out as much as possible, even if I didn't understand or agree with it. That might come later. But for now I wanted answers to many more questions.

While I was thinking about which question to ask next, Asne and Jacob cautioned me to pay attention for we were approaching a time warp. Jacob explained it as a time-space discontinuity. That is, at one moment you are in one time-space zone and when you cross a "magic" line and enter the time warp you are suddenly in another dimension.

"We are coming to it now and when we cross that line you'll find yourself in another world. Are you ready to come with us now? I hope you haven't changed your mind after hearing all that we have told you? If you want to come with us, now is the time. You remember we told you that we had made this long trip so that we could take you along and show you our world. Are you ready for it?"

They both looked at me.

"I'm ready!" I replied. "But can you tell me what I'll see where you're taking me? It's nice to know where I'm going so there won't be any surprises. What will it be like? What can I learn there? Is there anyone I can visit?"

"We'll take you to some lectures that will be of great interest to you. There are a number of pavilions which may fire your imagination, and there are so many historical figures there you can talk with and learn from. Besides I am sure you'll have a chance to see some people you knew when they were in the physical body."

"How do I get back?"

"We'll bring you back."

Asne and Jacob took my hands, and as soon as they did an electrifying impulse rushed through my body. As they raised their vibrations, and mine, we became a radiant shining light.

Before we started to cross the "magic" line, Jacob said "Let's go!" and we stepped into, what was to me, a very different environment. It definitely was not the familiar surroundings I knew so well. I was astounded and awed at what I saw. Here I was --- in a sparkling new world!

Chapter 3

A Sparkling New World

It had suddenly become very quiet, like right after a snowfall when everything appears to stand still. A deep, penetrating hush had fallen over the entire landscape. We had stepped into an awesome atmosphere where an Almighty Presence permeated everything. I was to learn that this Presence would prevail throughout our journey. I was afraid to say anything lest the solemn calm be disturbed. It was so peaceful and comforting that it gave me more energy than I had ever experienced before. The tranquillity wrapped itself around me and told me with an imperceptibly and quiet awareness not to be afraid.

This would be a new journey for me, and I knew it. Where it would lead I didn't have the slightest idea.

The sky was as clear as I had ever seen. But it wasn't blue. It was a color I couldn't describe, (something between a pink and yellow, all in pastels). It cast a pink-like glow over the entire scene. The stimulating air, with its captivating fragrance from all the flowers growing everywhere had a touch of elegance and friendliness. The whole environment felt so clean and pristine, like a clear crystal vase. I felt as though I could see into infinity.

I took a deep breath. It was like drinking a glass of pure water. As far as my eyes would take me I could see so clearly that everything seemed very close--almost within reach. I stood there in awe with my eyes absorbing the landscape, determined not to miss a thing.

My analytical mind tried to assess the situation for what it was, and not just for what I wanted it to be. It was like being in a beautiful foreign country, and not knowing what would come next.

I hadn't been much of an explorer at all. Exploration to me appeared as an unpleasant and very inconvenient undertaking. I'd just as soon do some research on a favorite subject or stay at home with a good book to read, or take a walk on the beach or watch a beautiful sunrise or sunset--or, if there was nothing else to do, to watch a good movie that would have some substance.

But to explore the unknown wasn't really my cup of soup. For exploration meant change to me, change in my outlook, attitudes and thinking patterns. And though all through my life I've gone through many changes of this sort, I still don't like the inner struggle that inevitably takes place during the process.

Something had to change, and I would rather not go into that subject unless I absolutely had to. Exploration and change: I had never taken the time to sort out these elements to determine if or where I could fit into such a scheme of things. In my younger days I had been a creature of habit; it was safer that way, something I could depend on, something that remained the same every day. Everything in its rightful place, so I knew where I could find it, be that in the area of engineering or religion. I considered myself to be a man of self-discipline and order.

Adventure, exploration and change: these three seemed to be undisciplined and disorderly to me. I wasn't entirely opposed to change, as long as it came at a convenient time and didn't disrupt my daily schedule. I had trained myself to make a habit of meeting schedules and reaching goals. That gave me a secure feeling, because then I knew where I was going. A look at the schedule would tell me that.

As a young man I was curious, a cautioned curiosity, wanting to investigate other knowledge in a logical, and orderly manner. In those days I had to follow a particular process, one step at a time, which eventually would take me to the desired goal. Whenever I had come into a situation I didn't understand, I wouldn't take one step ahead until I fully understood the present setting.

Over the years I had allowed myself to venture beyond the set patterns of belief and scientific dogmas. However, I hadn't been easy on myself. During these journeys of departures I had often been at odds with myself, wishing that the path I had chosen might be more acceptable to others. My process was at a snail's pace; but over the years I had made some progress, and this I have never regretted. However, in retrospect I did regret that I hadn't ventured out sooner, and at a faster pace.

Where I found myself now didn't give me any time or opportunity to question the whole situation. Asne and Jacob were in charge here, and I was satisfied to have them take the lead.

As a double Leo my first inclination in any situation has been a desire to step in and take charge, especially if the leadership seemed weak. But over the years I have learned to hold back unless requested to step in, and make suggestions when appropriate, allowing all concerned to learn from the process.

However, when in a new or strange situation, I always preferred to have a more experienced person lead the way, at least until I felt more comfortable in that environment.

Now here I was, having been invited to come along with Jacob and Asne to visit the "other side" of the veil. For a moment I wondered if I had been wise to accept this. I wished Doris could have been with me; it always made me feel more secure having her at my side. Doris has been my constant companion for many, many years, and I missed her sorely at this moment.

Then I felt Jacob's hand on my back gently pressing forward, and we began moving on ahead. Excitement for what I was to encounter replaced all other thoughts.

When we started to walk, I noticed there was no prepared road on which we could journey. I wondered if we were to travel over the fields, although that seemed not to be the easiest path to take.

But as soon as the first step was taken, a passage opened up, wide enough for us to walk side by side. The path was made available to us one step at a time. This, I thought, was intriguing.

Looking back I was even more surprised. For as we moved ahead the path behind us closed, leaving no trace of our ever having been there. We were walking on what seemed to me a magic path, and this was something new for me. I quickly saw the lesson in this.

Take one step at a time, in faith, and the path will open up. But in some situations it also closes so that no one can follow, or so that there can be no retreat. Each person, I mused, would be required to find his/her own way. The principle of faith, being accessible to everyone, is to be applied by each person individually. I was aware that in many other cases when a path is opened up, it remains open for others to follow. I didn't feel the need to have this lesson confirmed, so I said nothing to Asne and Jacob.

The landscape that rolled out before us was very different from what I was used to. The colors were vivid pastels, sparkling as if the whole landscape were dancing all around us. There was an abundance of flowers, large and small, in every conceivable color and shade, and of course there were roses and butterflies. The birds sang so much softer than I had ever heard, chirping quietly in harmony with each other. It struck me that perhaps they were afraid to disturb the tranquillity. But they had to sing; that's what birds do. Wherever I looked there was peace and serenity and nothing to disturb it. "What a heavenly sight," I thought. "I have never experienced anything like this before."

A Sparkling New World

The three of us walked in silence and I wondered where we were going, when--

"We're going to The Great Library, commonly known as the Akashic Records," Asne spoke up.

"I am familiar with the Akashic Records," I replied. "It will be interesting to visit that place under different circumstances. There is so much to learn there. I wonder if I will see my two guides where you are taking me; they have always been so helpful. I have visited there well over 7000 times.

"I would like to get you into a different section of The Great Library, but I'm not sure if I can. There you would see another part of this impressive structure and witness some of the events that take place there."

"Well, that would be very interesting, but while we're walking let's talk about why it's so easy for the two of you to read my mind," I said. "While I'm here, how can I block others from reading my mind? It is like my privacy has been invaded. I can't think the most innocent thoughts without you knowing what I'm thinking, even before I say or do anything. This can be very exasperating for me." I was waiting for an answer that would satisfy my curiosity and that would agree with my frustrations.

After a moment the answer came. "You can prevent others from reading your mind, but that means also that you can't read anybody else's mind either. It will be like isolating yourself. For here, we communicate by thought, and if there isn't anyone to communicate with, you'll live an isolated life.

"It's a two-way street or it is nothing. You can't have it both ways, reading the minds of others and preventing them from reading yours. That's not the kind of life we recommend you'd want to live, anyway. For right here, where we are now, the opportunities are open for you to learn and grow.

"Just look over there," Asne pointed to the right where a number of people were sitting. They all had their backs turned to each other, not wanting to have anything to do with anyone."

"Is that all they have to do here?" I asked. I was wondering why so many people had isolated themselves in thought from everybody. "Is this affliction widespread?"

"It's a well known blight on planet Earth," Asne replied. "That's where these souls came from. If they don't open their minds, it will be so much more difficult for them to eventually learn. There is a principle which says, 'The mind is like a parachute; it functions only when open.' It's a mystery to many on this and other levels of Heaven why some souls won't get along with other souls. This will have to stop sometime; otherwise it will only lead to contention and war on Earth." She spoke emphatically, underlining every word with decisive gestures.

The three of us watched these souls sitting there in silence, and wondered how much longer it would continue. It was such a pitiful sight, but no one forced them to behave like that. It was what they chose to do, and they were experiencing the consequences of their decision.

Asne said that they had just arrived, had no intentions of following the directions that their Messenger of Light had offered, and refused to recognize that they were no longer in their physical bodies on Earth. They saw no need to change their attitudes and way of living. Their philosophy, which they had practiced on Earth was, "Why change when we can maintain the status quo?" There was every indication that they intended to live up to that philosophy, no matter where they were. They had to defend their belief system and to a great extent they had lived their lives with that philosophy.

Most people like this had aspirations to grow and become spiritual giants, but weren't willing to recognize that without change it was impossible to grow on any level. Misery loves company; so as long as they stayed together here, they wouldn't have to believe that their way of life was faulty. They were determined that life would continue on as it always had been--so they thought.

"You will notice that all of these groups are outside of the Great Library, and have not entered yet for their review and indoctrination. They have refused to go any further. Here in Heaven souls aren't forced to learn and grow, for we know that learning and growing cannot be legislated. Very often there are some very violent discussions among these types of souls, each wanting to prove a point and come out winning. None of them have realized that it isn't a matter of winning, but of learning to live. They aren't yet ready to learn and to grow.

"Just because a soul makes the transition," Asne continued, "doesn't mean that it will know any more than when it was on Earth. From what I know, these groups haven't even checked in yet, and who knows for how long they will remain in their rebellious and confused state of mind. Therefore, as long as they refuse to check in, they can't receive any help. Everything here is strictly on a voluntary basis. You can make your own choices; however, you can't return to Earth unless you have been cleared by your guides."

"Well, how do you get cleared?" I inquired.

This query from me prompted memories in Asne of how curious she was when she first arrived some years ago.

Her own experience upon arrival was that of wonderment, awe and curiosity. She was eager to follow the guide who took charge of her, and explained to her all she needed to know for the time being. She asked so many questions that her guide was just about worn out by the time she was through with her orientation and indoctrination. While going through the reviews in The Great Library, she noticed how much clearer her memory was since leaving her physical body behind. Everything now was so crystal clear and there was no forgetting. This was both good and disturbing.

To remember the good things is very pleasant, but to recall those situations and events that were painful and embarrassing was simply not uplifting or inspiring. But on the other hand these disturbing memories could serve as a reminder that there were many things that needed to be worked on, and many things to be set right when the opportunity was made available. Whenever she got back to Earth (her guides had told her that she would return some day) she would have to make a more concentrated and dedicated effort to balance the books. Before she returned to Earth, she had been advised to take some courses in spiritual accounting.

Inwardly she sighed, for she dreaded the very thought of returning to a place where there was so much hatred and discontent. She would have liked to stay right where she was, but knew that in doing so she would deny herself any chance of getting beyond her own prejudices and resentments.

She had been told time and again to store in her mind the instructions she received so that she could put them into action when she was given another physical body. She wondered how she would do when that time ever came. Right now she felt like an "arm-chair general," just talking about the challenges and not having yet entered into the battles of working them out.

Asne enjoyed showing me this first level of Heaven. She had observed and learned these procedures for a number of years. This was all familiar territory to her.

"Did you understand my question?" I persisted.

"Excuse me," Asne apologized. "I was remembering how curious I was when I came here. Instead of having me tell you how people are cleared, perhaps before you leave I can show you. In fact, Jacob can show you just as easily. But we'll come to the first station very shortly, and then you'll know a little more. So have a little patience," she remarked.

That was all the patience I had--very little. Yet I knew I had to wait for the answers and that irked me. For years I had either found the answers myself or I would ask those in the know. I never wanted long and complicated discourses. I wanted answers that were short and to the point. If they were more complicated and difficult to understand than the questions I asked, which sometimes had happened, I'd just as soon drop the whole matter for the time being and try to figure it out on my own, which in the long run, of course, would take much longer. But that's the kind of person I was.

We followed the magical path which eventually took us to an immense building, made from glistening white marble. The sight of it was very familiar to me. It was a huge structure and well maintained. Large and beautiful plants from all parts of the universe formed an exquisite landscape. There were typical English gardens and Japanese rock gardens with artistically manicured Bonsai trees. There were displays typifying French horticulture, Spanish and Italian, as well as from every country and culture in the entire world and beautiful unfamiliar displays which must have come from other star systems. There weren't any groundskeepers seen, so I wondered who took care of these plants and flowers. The maintenance alone would cost a small fortune, and the water bill would no doubt be enormous.

"Well, what do you think of it?" Asne inquired. "This is the place where all who have made the transition come to first. Everybody has to pass through here before they are assigned to their classrooms and begin to work on their lessons. As you can imagine, this is a busy place. People arrive here at all times from every part of the universe.

"Sometimes it is busier here than at other times, such as when there is a war on planet Earth. Many of those who arrive from such violent events are angry or hurt, and usually completely disoriented. They are literally basket cases.

"Fortunately there are a number of specially trained counselors who come to their aid as soon as they arrive, and they are taken to a section in the library reserved for such cases. There they are counseled and encouraged to go on with the next phase of their lives, which will take place on this plane and will require an undetermined length of time to accomplish.

"A similar procedure takes place when suicides arrive. They are still in the same frame of mind as when they were on Earth, and are very disappointed because the problems they had hoped to escape are still with them.

"As you know there are counselors here who are specifically assigned to work only with suicides. This, of course, is a very difficult mission, but it can prove to be exceedingly rewarding.

"Another special group of counselors are the ones who will come to the rescue of those who have made the transition because of accidents, like an automobile collision. These counselors also have a very difficult task; in fact--" and she interrupted herself, "just look over there," she pointed straight ahead, "and you'll see what I mean."

An elderly man was greeting a newly arrived young couple who on their honeymoon had been killed in a car crash. They just stood there as though they couldn't believe what had happened. Both of them shook their heads and blinked their eyes, hoping that what they had experienced was only a dream, and that soon they would wake up and continue on their honeymoon. The counselor didn't let them stay there too long. Walking between them he put his hands on their shoulders, and silently they strolled to an area where the young couple would be counseled so they could accept the situation for what it was.

Outside of the huge library structure colossal crowds were gathered, and over a public address system instructions were given to the crowd to line up in front of the letter which corresponded to the first letter of their last name (that is, the name they had used before they departed from planet Earth, or other planets in the universe). It looked like a scene from a college registration day. However, they all knew this was no college admission process. It was far more serious than that.

In silence, one by one each stepped up to the large designated tables and gave his or her name. After the official at the table had made a thorough check, each new arrival received a large book and was directed to go inside. I observed the books, for they seemed to be familiar to me. They were all leather bound in attractive colors, with pages edged in gold. These were similar to the kind of books I had worked with when I went to the Akashic Records to obtain information for the thousands of people who had requested my services.

I assumed that these souls who were about to enter the Great Library had received their own book of life, and now were to study it so that they could learn from their own experiences. However, I wanted confirmation on that so I turned quietly and thoughtfully to Asne and Jacob and asked, "Have I perceived this scene correctly? Namely that the books that these souls have received are their own Book of Life from which they can now learn as they review it?"

Asne quickly answered my question. "You have made a good observation. I'm sure you already know that all souls who enter here are given their own Book of Life to study and learn from. In a way this is judgment time for them. I know that you are familiar with what is written by Paul the Apostle regarding this: that everyone shall appear before the judgment seat to be judged according to what the soul has done, whether it be good or evil. In this way they are their own judges being judged by the deeds they have done.

"This is a very serious time for them. They have to search themselves and determine what errors have been committed, and try to correct these in their next incarnation. The good deeds they had done will help them make better choices, and not fall for the temptations to which they had become involved. In reviewing the events in their own books, they will also recognize the poor choices they have made. As they are reading their own story, the past and the present is laid out before them, and if they are observant and try to remember all the information, they would have something powerful to work with when they return to planet Earth.

"You see," Asne continued, "each soul, upon arrival, deposits at The Great Library a copy of its own record from the immediate past life. This is added to what the soul deposited after each of the previous lives. As it studies its own Book of Life, it is facing itself and its deeds.

"You're aware of the statement that says it is appointed for all once to die and after that the judgment. All these people have died and are now judging themselves as they review their own book of life and examine their own past lives. This process is repeated life after life until the soul finally has matured."

"By the way," Jacob broke in, "you need to be aware that nobody knows that we have brought you here. Don't make yourself known to anybody before we have a chance to obtain official permission for your visit; otherwise you could cause a minor disturbance. Follow us and don't talk to anyone; don't touch anyone or anything. Just follow us and hold your questions until later."

I understood and agreed to follow their instructions.

Asne now explained to me that there were separate entrances on this side of the building for each letter of the alphabet. "This facilitates the crowds very efficiently" she explained.

"Well," I said thoughtfully "although for 25 years while I made daily journeys to the Akashic records, I have never seen these entrances before. The access I used was always like a private entrance. No one else was there except me and my guides. Why the difference?"

"You came to The Great Library, or the Akashic Records, as you call it, for a different purpose than all these souls you see entering the building," Jacob explained. "You went to the Akashic Records to obtain information for people who are still on the Earth plane, to help them grow and get on with their lives. A different approach to the building was made available to you for that reason. As you told us, you were the only one entering the Akashic Records at that time. The reason for that was so that you wouldn't be distracted from your mission by the presence of other souls, except for your guides.

"The souls you have seen who were given certain books have a different purpose. They are here to learn from their own experiences, deeds or misdeeds, and have the opportunity to confer with other souls who are in similar life-reviewing circumstances, and hopefully try to learn something. I'm sure you understand this, don't you?"

I nodded and replied, "Yes I do."

Asne and Jacob were now conferring with each other about a matter. After a lengthy discussion between the two of them, Asne turned to me and confided that they had come up with a plan, but weren't sure if it would work. I questioned why a plan was necessary, because I really didn't understand what was going on. I asked for an explanation, but evidently there wasn't any time for that.

"Wait here with Jacob. I'll be back as soon as I can." Looking at me she emphasized in a staccato voice: "Don't - go - anywhere - and - don't - talk - to - anyone - or - touch - anything. You understand?" I nodded my head. Not because I agreed, but because I didn't know what might happen if I didn't follow her orders.

With that she hurriedly found her way to The Great Library and disappeared in the sea of people.

I wondered where she had gone and what was going on.

Jacob looked at me and smiled, "Asne has gone to find out if it is possible to obtain a full day's pass for you. I have no idea if she'll be successful in that, so we'll just have to wait until she returns. We'll both know by then."

"What'll happen if she isn't able to get a pass for me?"

"We'll have to take you back to where you came from."

"But that would mean I wouldn't be able to see anything or talk to anyone. Is that what might happen?" I asked rapidly, indicating concern and worry.

"That's right," Jacob answered. "It won't do you any good to worry, Aron, or to be concerned about the matter. It is out of your hands. All we can do now is to wait."

Jacob's appearance hadn't changed at all since Doris and I visited him in Norway in 1974. We had been on a trip to Europe when we stopped over in Trondheim to visit my mother and other family members. Jacob had come for lunch, and as usual he was very quiet. Now and then he would make a few short comments in the conversation, but mostly he would just listen to the others at the table. His hair was very thin, then and it still was. His light blue eyes had the same melancholy and far-away look as it had for many years. It was as if he were still piercing the future, the past trailing along with him. His speech was slow, as it had been in the past, weighing every word on his scale of wisdom and understanding. His slender figure was the same as it had always been, giving a picture of youth and vitality.

Jacob was right, there wasn't anything else to do but wait. It was obvious that Jacob wasn't concerned about the matter, but I was. I knew that I wasn't supposed to be here in the first place, as Asne had made that abundantly clear to me. I looked at Jacob a little nervously, not knowing what the next few moments would reveal.

I certainly wouldn't want to leave this place, not just now. There was so much I wanted to know; so I thought I'd better ask Jacob a few questions just in case I had to leave without being shown around. I supposed that since Jacob had been in Heaven for several years he surely would know some of the answers. But there wasn't any time for questions. I was thinking that this is a strange new world, and wondered what was coming next. We didn't have to wait long.

Asne came running toward us waving a piece of paper and smiling from ear to ear. Within ear shot she shouted, "I got it! I got it!"

She spoke excitedly, and being short of breath the words came haltingly, "I--obtained a full--day's--visitor's pass--for you, Aron. Aren't you excited?"

Without waiting for me to respond she went on. "I had to talk real fast and convincingly before they would listen to me. I explained to the one in charge what type of work you are doing, and how useful it might be for you to see some of the activities here. At first he wasn't very impressed, and stressed that no visitors had ever been allowed to stay a full day.

"I was reminded time and again that I had a very unusual request, and when he checked through the records he confirmed that no one had ever received a full day's pass. He was so hard-headed and stubborn, I didn't think I'd ever convince him that this was a different case altogether. When he asked in what way this case was so different from all the others. I told him that the pass was for my brother. That didn't make any impression on him whatsoever, and I was ready to leave when all of a sudden he gave his approval. I was so surprised! I could hardly believe that he had finally agreed to issue this pass for you!

"For an entire day we will open doors for you to worlds unknown. It will be breathtaking and very delightful. So now we can proceed. Ready?" Without saying anything further, she led the way to our first stop.

Chapter 4

The Akashic Records

We passed through the masses assembled in front of the Great Library and approached the first large table. When the official saw the three of us, he motioned for us to go to the end of the line. We were told that everything had to be done in an orderly manner, and nothing was to interfere with the already long established and proven policy. He had his orders from higher authority. When we didn't follow his orders, he asked why.

Asne waved the one-day pass in front of him. She knew that this pass would give them special privileges while they escorted me around. She had been told by the issuing agent that such a pass was a rarity; so she should consider herself having accomplished something very special.

The official took it, studied it on both sides, mumbled something, and called several associates over. They all looked it over thoroughly, studying it as if it were a treasure map. After they were finished, they started again, discussing the whole matter between them in a very low voice. It was impossible to hear what they had to say, so there was no way of telling what their decision would be. Then something happened.

One of them pointed to the signature at the bottom of the pass, and they all became speechless. It was as if they were listening to someone or something. Then they mumbled to each other, "This is very unusual." We could hear that. Without another word each one turned with a shrug of his shoulders, leaving the official to handle the situation.

I observed all this with great interest. What they had seen I thought must have been something of real importance; maybe something that they had never seen before or perhaps had only heard about from others.

Slowly and with great respect the official turned to Asne. In a deep, solemn voice he declared that everything was in order. She could proceed with her guest to the office that would issue a temporary pass for me. The pass was necessary, he explained. Then he made us understand that in case we got separated during my visit then I, having the proper identification (the pass), could ask for directions so that I could be re-united with my sister and brother.

"Make sure you present this," and he waved the pass authorization in front of Asne. "This piece of paper is a collector's item, just look at that signature," and excitedly he pointed directly to it. "I have never seen that signature before, and I doubt that many ever have. It sure would be worth your while if you could convince those in charge at the pass office if you could keep it, and frame it for a display when friends come to visit. But unfortunately you'll have to surrender it for the temporary pass. You can move on." He motioned us toward a door that automatically opened up.

With Asne leading the way we entered The Great Library. As soon as we were on the inside, the door closed without a sound. We were in a courtyard that led to another door with a sign reading "Pass Issuing Office."

Inside Asne presented the pass authorization to the person behind the counter, who looked at it very closely. Then the clerk called over several other office workers who also studied it. They discussed among themselves what this meant, and what they should do about it. The scene was a repetition of what had taken place earlier.

"We have decided to follow the directive on this authorization and issue to you," and the official looked at me, "a temporary pass, valid for one day only. With this pass you are free to go anywhere, in the company of your sister and brother. You may observe anything you want. You can attend any class that is in session, ask any question that you so desire of the teacher, and talk to anybody you see outside the class room setting. We think this experience here will be very helpful to you.

"But there is one area where you may only observe. That is the admission facility for new arrivals. There is to be no disturbance of the proceedings that take place there. If you cause any disturbance, this pass will immediately be revoked and you'll be "escorted" back to where you came from. Understood?"

I nodded. "But," I asked, "a one day pass just won't give me enough time to explore and learn. A one day pass is hardly adequate for what I want to know. Don't you agree?" I looked for an agreement from the official.

"You must understand, sir," the clerk replied in a stern voice "the circumstances of your visit are very unusual. A visit such as yours is very rare. You are most fortunate to be allowed to obtain even a one day pass. You'll find that this pass will give you more than enough time to accumulate the knowledge you need for the present."

"You're right," I quickly agreed. "A one day pass is just fine. I feel very privileged to receive this permit."

"Now, if you'll step over here," she directed, "we'll take your picture with our latest high technology camera, and your pass will be finished sooner than you can blink an eye."

I followed her over to a camera that looked more like a cylindrical, narrow tube. There were no visible lenses such as that which a normal camera would have. I became excited to see how such a camera would work. I quickly looked around the room and noticed that there were a number of these cylindrical tubes pointed at me.

"Now, please step up to the green line painted on the floor so that your toes touch the line. Then look up and try to smile. O.K.?"

I followed the instructions, placing my toes so that they just touched the green line. I looked up, smiled, and the picture was taken. In less than a second the finished pass came out through a chute, and I was told to slip the attached band around my neck. I was amazed.

"It takes one-five hundredth of a second to take the picture and develop it," the clerk explained. "Another one-one thousandth of a second to laminate it and attach a band. It takes the longest time to send the picture down the chute, therefore we're working on an updated model to make it even faster.

"Look at your picture and you will see it is a hologram. Turn it to the backside and there is the back of your head. Now look at it on one end and you will see a side view of yourself. That's why all the cameras are placed around you, as you no doubt have already noticed. On the opposite end of your pass you will see the other side view. There is a complete description of you on that pass. Your eyes can be enlarged so that the proper healers can examine them and know what's wrong with you, should you require such assistance while you are here. Everything about you is encoded in that pass, and there isn't anything we don't know about you.

"By the way, most souls who come to this office to obtain temporary passes are those who live here, and they have obtained permission to visit other levels of Heaven. It isn't often that someone who lives on planet Earth is granted a pass even for a day to visit this level."

"I will now turn you over to Justin who will tell you where your next stop will be." With that she gestured toward a gentleman sitting behind a large desk that had many buttons and lights on it. To say the least it looked very impressive.

The three of us approached him and he stood up to greet us. While we were being seated, he moved his hand over the desk, and looking at me said with a smile, "All this is impressive, isn't it?" He had, of course, read my mind.

"I am here to acquaint you with what you will experience at your next stop," he began, "so let me have your undivided attention.

"You will be led into a large hall, which being square in shape is so huge you won't be able to see the walls. You will be met by an escort who will explain in detail, if you so desire, what's going on. This place will be filled with newly arrived souls working on their first assignments. You will notice that each soul will have a personal guide to help it finish its task as soon as possible. This first assignment as you will later discover, is a very important one for all of them.

"This is all you need to know for the time being. So if the three of you will go through the door on your left, you may proceed."

"While I remember it, here is a map of the area of the first Heaven. This will give you an indication of how large this place is. It also gives you some points of interest which you undoubtedly would like to visit, like the Museum and the Time Machine exhibit; and by all means don't miss the most interesting and busiest pavilion of all, called Karma Are Us."

With that Justin got up from his desk, and pointing towards the door, he bid us good-bye. "If you get lost, consult the map that I gave you."

We shook hands and walked to the designated door. As though on signal it opened up for us and we stepped through the doorway. A guide approached us and introduced herself as Renee.

"While you're here at your first stop, I will be your guide. If you have any questions, I shall be glad to answer them, provided there is an answer available. But first, observe and try to understand for yourself what's going on." All the while she spoke in a soft whisper.

We had come into a jumbo-sized library. There were bookshelves as high as the eye could see and far beyond, and just as long. I observed the distance between the bookshelves to be at least 20-30 feet. Although I had seen this room thousands of times, I was always impressed with its immense size! There were books of every conceivable size and color. Some of the shelves were almost empty of books because they were being used by the new arrivals, whereas other shelves were quite filled.

The entire library was wrapped in deep silence, although the huge room was filled with people. The four of us took a tour through this enormous room.

Books are one of my weaknesses. Whenever I visit a bookstore, I invariably buy a book or two to read when I have time. Usually, I turn my head the other way when I pass a bookstore so that I won't be tempted to go in. (I recently counted the volumes in my personal library, and found that I have over 2000 books.)

The library was filled with light and a wonderful fragrance of roses. The guide suggested we take advantage of the balcony where we could have a better overall view of the area. Here we observed the souls in deep thought as they read information from a monitor in front of them. They seemed to confer often with their counselor/guides, who were seated next to them. Renee explained that the newly arrived souls are reviewing the events from the life they had just left. This will be presented to them as a journal, one that they will take with them to work on in their classes. That information will be added to the journal of their other past lives.

"It's a complicated process because it isn't easy to remember every little detail of every event, together with the emotions, likes and dislikes, joys and sorrows, anger, disappointment, frustration, denial and acceptance." Renee explained.

"In addition, every opportunity taken advantage of or missed will be brought to their attention, including what they did and shouldn't have done, and what they didn't do and should have. Fear and courage come to light just as it was exhibited in life. Everything that has been kept secret will now be uncovered."

At that point I was reminded of the words of the Master, "For nothing is secret that shall not be made manifest."

"What they're undertaking can at times be very embarrassing or devastating, but they are surrounded in love. If they are to learn their spiritual lesson, it has to be brought out now, so that they can use their own background, successes and failures as a textbook for themselves. What better way is there to learn but from their own experiences? This process can take as long as needed, for it has to be complete, and very accurate.

"Take a good look at each soul, and see what you can discover," Renee challenged me. I studied as many people as I could, seeing nothing unusual except that each were wearing a white headband. On their table was a monitor, and next to each person was a counselor/guide. I reported that to Renee, admitting that I didn't know why each was fitted with a headband.

"It is more than a decoration," she informed me. "It is a magnetic pick-up that adjusts itself automatically to the frequencies of the brain waves. This, as you may recognize, is a highly sophisticated and greatly advanced technology you are witnessing in operation. I am proud to inform you that this is also the latest model; we just received it three days ago. All of our technology is updated every six months. If all goes well on planet Earth, you may have this technology in operation within the next few years. Interesting, isn't it? But let me go on with my explanation.

"While the new arrivals are reviewing the events in their lives, information is retrieved from their brain cells through the magnetic sensors located in the headband. This information is displayed on the monitor in front of them. This is identical to a computer processing information so that it can be read or printed out. Like a computer this is also a non-destructive retrieval. This is a provision to aid the souls in recording all events from their immediate past lives. What they can't or won't remember is displayed on the monitor so that they can bring to mind events that may have been important to them and from which they can further learn.

"You will notice that there are several large books at each desk. These are books which contain a comprehensive and detailed account of all that has been experienced by that person up to this point. This information is deposited in their personal set of books after each of their incarnations. If they continue to return to Earth more books will of course be added. You would be amazed how many times the same mistakes are made over and over again. Still, when the souls can read their own records, they can more readily recognize lessons they failed to learn. Then they are better prepared to work on improving these aspects of their lives.

"The most important aspect of this exercise is for the person to learn from past mistakes, so as not to repeat them in the next life; also to learn from their successes and move on to greater achievements.

"Then when they have completed this assignment, which turns out to be more than just a term paper, they will have the opportunity to review and study the events from their immediate past lives.

"As you can imagine, not everybody agrees with what is displayed on the monitor, some will argue with their guides about the accuracy of what they see. The consistent remark is that something is wrong with the monitor, or the pick-up probe, or perhaps both. Sometimes the disagreement about the accuracy of their accounts can be very emotionally argued. Some of the newly arrived try very hard to convince their guides that the monitors aren't giving an accurate account of what took place, and that it wasn't their fault that all these things went so badly. Why should they be blamed for what went wrong? And this is just a small sample of all the 'interesting' events we come across here," Renee explained.

She looked over the scene going on below, and after a while spotted an episode which had the potential of blossoming out into a serious situation. A man had started to argue with his counselor/guide over the supposed inaccuracy of what the monitor indicated. It became obvious to Renee that something very interesting might be developing. Turning to me and pointing in the direction of the potential explosion, she asked me if I would be interested in listening to the conversation. I said I would.

"We aren't permitted to leave this position of observation to listen," she assured me. "We can hear the conversation right where we are through this unique listening device. It is a high frequency, low power, laser transmitter/receiver which transmits a colorless, beam over long distances. The beam is voice modulated and voice activated so we can hear everything that's being said. It can follow, like in your case on Earth, the curvature of the terrain, or travel around corners or in a straight line by programming the transmitter, either before or during transmission. A monitor, which is part of the device, keeps the operator in touch with the beam so it can be re-directed if and when that is necessary or required. This beam has intelligence and can communicate with the operator. Let me show you how it works."

With that she brought out a small device, no larger than a cordless telephone with a built-in monitor. "This is truly portable, weighs one half pound, including the power source, and the monitor can be removed and expanded into a larger screen."

She demonstrated this by removing the monitor from its original position in the hand set, and seemingly without any effort using her hands stretched it to a larger size and then attached it with an adhesive to the laser transmitter/ receiver.

Renee positioned the device in the direction of the potential explosive event, turned on the equipment and motioned to me to listen. All this time Asne and Jacob were watching in the background. They had been through this indoctrination and didn't want to interfere with Renee's demonstration.

I listened, but motioned to Renee that I could hear nothing but noise. She quickly made a small adjustment that made a big difference.

"Why is it always my fault?" I began to hear. "Why should I be blamed for all the difficulties I got into? As you know, I never admitted to any mistakes, but it was because I never made any! I want the readout on this monitor changed to comply with what I have remembered, because that's the truth the way I see it. Besides, I know there is something wrong with this machine."

The one speaking turned to his counselor/guide for agreement. "I want another machine that is working properly, and I'll prove to you that I am right."

"But Felipe, we have already changed our monitors four times, and they have all given the identical information as you see now displayed. Isn't it time that you recognize the mistakes you've made in your past lives, and time to admit that you haven't always been right? You and I have been over the same material time and again, and it is quite obvious that you don't want to face up to the truth."

"Don't blame me, I haven't done anything wrong." Felipe insisted, showing signs of exasperation. "Why is it that nobody understands me? No wonder I have been a martyr in so many lives. If you," and he looked at his counselor/guide, "could only have some patience, like me, you would see where I am right and always have been."

The guide rolled his eyes in disbelief. "How much longer will this charade go on?" he responded.

"What charade?" Felipe defended himself. "I'm telling the truth about myself. Always have and always will!" And after a short pause "Why is it so important anyway to be so accurate about these little details? I think that an approximation should be sufficient. Don't you agree?"

"Definitely not! Unless you know all the details about your behavior, you'll never know how to improve your life and personality, and you'll be repeating the same miserable mistakes life after life, just like you've been doing for too many lifetimes already. It is time for a change. We have discussed this issue long enough and for far too many times. If you don't become agreeable to the necessary changes in your life, I'll just have to call on your sister for assistance, and you know what that means, don't you?"

Felipe became silent for a while. (At this point Renee picked up his thoughts and relayed them to me.). He thought of his sister and their relationship. It hadn't been very cordial. For the most part they had argued a great deal whenever she had tried to help him see the error in his tendency to blame others for his own many mistakes. Time and again, in a kind but firm and determined way, she had pointed out to him that he was irresponsible for the way he conducted himself, believing that he wasn't accountable to anybody, not even himself.

His sister Renee was the oldest in the family of six children, and she felt keenly the responsibility in caring for her younger brothers and sisters after her parents were arrested and executed for sabotage by the Germans during World War II. Suddenly they were orphans. With the help of friends and relatives they were able to hide until the war was over.

"Felipe was able to be educated as an engineer," Renee explained, and obtained a good position with the government of France. But the tragedy of losing his parents had made an indelible impression on his psyche. He blamed the Germans, and rightly so, for the loss of his father and mother.

"After that, he found it convenient to blame the Germans for his difficulty in adjusting to the hard life he was forced to lead as an orphan. From then on he always found someone else to blame for his problems. His two failed marriages were blamed on his wives. He was thinking of getting married a third time when he was killed in an automobile accident. His last words were, "The other driver is at fault and he prevented me from getting married." Actually, he was driving at high speed on the wrong side of the highway, having just left his bride-to-be in a rage after a violent argument.

"I preceded him in death by several years, " Renee went on, "having died from a lung disease contracted during the war. I was waiting for him when he arrived here, hoping that he would have changed. But there was no sign of any improvement in his disposition.

"It took me a long time to convince him that he needed to get on with his education in life, which meant he had to present himself at the Great Library, where he would receive further instructions as to what he should do.

"There he was assigned to a guide who would work with him initially until he had reviewed his journal and placed it in a permanent volume." At this point Renee pointed me back to Felipe.

"Well, what will it be?" the guide prodded Felipe. "Are you going to follow my suggestions, or shall I call on your sister? You have one minute to make up your mind."

"But tell me," Felipe interjected, "what good will this journal do me anyway? Nobody will pay any attention to my side of the story. My life isn't for publication anyway."

"On that you can rely," his guide replied. "No one here will pay attention to your side of the story because you have distorted the facts. Your own brain waves have recorded the truth. What you see on the monitor is what your brain waves have put there. The reason you are to record the events from your past life is so that those facts about you can become part of your larger volume, which stores the events you have recorded when you returned here after your many other past lives. That will give you an opportunity, when needed, or when you are directed to do so, to return here and read about how you reacted or responded to situations and what attitudes you held. In that way you may have an opportunity to learn and perhaps mature a little.

"Right now you are like a spoiled child. You see, Felipe, what you have observed before, and what you are observing now on the monitor, is your own personal book of life. It is there for your benefit, and only you can open up your book. You lived it; you wrote it; and you'll hopefully learn from it. This is your ticket to a better and more meaningful life. I'm sure you understand how important this work is for you. You're going to learn from yourself, being both the teacher and the student."

Felipe saw the light. Or perhaps he gave up trying to do it his way, because he knew he couldn't get away with it anymore. Turning to his guide he agreed to accept what he read on the monitor.

Renee turned off the device, and motioned to us to follow her to the next station.

I spoke quietly. "Is he making any progress?"

"A little," she responded. "He has so much to learn. But then, all of us have that challenge, don't we?"

She took us over to a large aerial photograph of a building that had many sides to it. It looked a little like the Pentagon in Washington D.C., but much larger.

"This is a picture of The Great Library, the building we are in, and," pointing to a spot, explained, "we are right here. This structure has seven sides to it, and there is a reason for that. Each of the seven sides is so huge that you can't see another side unless you are near a corner. Each side has a Grecian architecture. You may not realize this, but this building is taller than your Empire State Building, the Sears Tower, and the Statue of Liberty combined, and that takes in only the first section. There is more above that.

"The reason for the seven sides is that the first side is the entrance for new arrivals; that's the side the three of you entered. The second side is an exit when the newly arrived have finished their journals and it has been placed in a permanent volume. The third side is an entrance for those who need to return to the Great Library to study their own records, and of course the fourth side is the exit for these souls. This exit takes them to another area for learning and contemplation.

"The fifth side is both an entrance and exit for some of those from Earth who are learning to read the Records. Those who come for the initial instructions in learning how to read the records arrive on a porch-like verandah where their guides are waiting for them. They are escorted into the part of the Great Library set aside for this work, and their guides are watching them very carefully during this part of their training.

"The sixth side is the entrance I use," I said.

"I know," Renee agreed. "This sixth side contains the entrance and exit for those who are making the same effort. Here, however, the readers arrive at the bottom of a long stairway made of marble, and at the top the guides will be waiting for them. These guides do not go with the readers into the

Library. It is assumed that they know what to do, otherwise they wouldn't be allowed to use this entrance.

"The guides are there to encourage the readers. At times they may have some personal messages for them, but should the readers find themselves in trouble, they will suggest ways by which they can come to a solution for their problem. By the way, as you know, readers with high integrity will never knowingly open the records of Earth dwellers without obtaining their permission from them, or in the case of children, from their parents. The seventh side is the exit for the souls who are returning to Earth to experience another incarnation.

"We have a very orderly system here, and it functions quite well. Sometimes there is congestion at the exit doors, but the attendants on duty quickly bring order out of the confusion.

"Now, let me show you where your next visit will be," Renee continued, directing my attention to a very interesting map. It showed a large area outside The Great Library with many buildings, parks and large courtyard areas. It was clear that The Great Library was the only way of entrance to this area.

"By touching any buildings on the map," she went on, "a description will come up showing what classes are conducted there, the length of instruction, who the teacher is, and what the pre-requisites are to attend these classes. Of course, all classes are available for everybody provided they have first attended certain basic instructions. Attendance at these classes is voluntary, but greatly encouraged. Naturally, visitors are exempted from the requisites."

Pointing to the map again, she suggested a few places that might be of interest to me. "Before you return to Earth, and if there is time, you must visit the Museum, The Time Machine, and of course the most popular pavilion of them all"--she made a dramatic pause--"Karma Are Us."

She turned to me and said that her part of the tour was now finished, and that I, together with Jacob and Asne, could leave this area and explore other points of interest. She reminded me not to get lost, to refer to the map if I did, or ask for directions. And by all means not to lose or misplace my one day pass.

"Any questions?" She hoped there wouldn't be any. But knowing how people are she had an intuitive feeling that she was dead wrong. And she was right!

"A lot of people think," I began, "that when a soul crosses over from life on the Earth plane to this heavenly plane, all of a sudden it knows everything there is to know. Would you comment on that?"

"You may recall what you observed regarding my brother and the conversation between him and his counselor. All who arrive here are no smarter or wiser, nor have they any more knowledge than when they lived on Earth. If you lived a generous life on Earth, you will arrive here with the same attitude. A negative or selfish life on Earth will manifest itself in that way upon arrival on this side.

"Most souls, when they first arrive here, feel so good in this wonderful environment that they believe all knowledge is imparted to them. But of course it isn't so. Having instant knowledge doesn't do anything for the growth of the soul. You learn sometimes by trial and error, through discipline and order or following your inner guidance, and especially by applying principles. Applying principles develops wisdom.

"Going through the process of growing can be painful and frustrating; it can also be very exciting. But then, every soul travels on its own path. It can be similar and/or parallel to others, nevertheless it is still its own. You can learn on both sides of the veil. The opportunities are placed before you with a good selection of challenges. Just because a soul has a difficult life on Earth doesn't mean that the soul isn't growing.

"Another matter you might like to know about is that although a soul may have reached a very high state of spirituality and service, that doesn't mean that it will always remain there. There is no such thing as seniority or security in this system. There is a need to continually learn and to grow spiritually. If a soul of high development should get itself involved in some questionable negative activities, that soul could very well fall from its pinnacle and end up on square one, thus having to start all over again."

"But is that fair?" I questioned. "Look at how long a soul may have worked on its development. Making one mistake in one life shouldn't have to put it in such jeopardy that it has to start all over again?"

"It depends on the severity of the situation," Renee explained. "It isn't one mistake that puts a soul in jeopardy. No one is perfect. Keep in mind that the more light a soul has, or the higher a soul has developed, the more responsibility is placed upon it.

"Of course, if the soul makes amends, forgives or asks for forgiveness for what it has done, the damage may not be too great. Nevertheless, the scars from the wrongdoing are still in the soul, like nail marks left in a fine piece of wood after the nails have been removed. I hope this answers your question. Anything else you'd like to know, don't hesitate to ask the teacher in the classrooms where you visit."

With that she directed us to the exit door, and left us on our own.

Chapter 5

Look Who's Coming to Heaven

O utside the Great Library we found ourselves in a huge open plaza paved with white marble tile. Souls were excitedly discussing the latest news about who would be arriving. Relatives were waiting at the exit doors of The Great Library where their loved ones were completing their journals.

Although the relatives were well acquainted with the process for new arrivals, yet they were eager to acquaint them with their new environment.

Asne and Jacob informed me of the soon arrival of a particular soul, Flavius Flatonia. A sizable number of welcoming souls had already gathered at his arrival gate. News of his coming had been posted on the bulletin boards. It had caused quite a stir among the large number of fundamentalists who knew of Flavius for a period of several years when they were on planet Earth. These souls were here to learn that love is more important than agreement. They were still under the bondage of some of their old established dogmas and creeds.

Asne explained that rumors had it that these souls were planning to descend upon the plaza in force to see if they could prevent Flavius from gaining entrance. She and Jacob wanted me to understand why there might be an extra large influx of souls coming into the plaza all at once.

Sure enough, suddenly many souls began coming in from the outskirts of the plaza.

I exclaimed, "I see what you mean!" As the three of us waited, the crowd was heading toward gate "L". We could overhear some of their conversations.

Some of them were discussing the horrors of Hell and how happy they were for being in a place where it was so pleasant. But everyone in that crowd had been horrified when the announcement was posted that Flavius Flatonia had arrived. When he had completed the initial process in The Great Library, he would appear at exit door "L," an abbreviation for "LOVE."

A big band started to play a well rehearsed welcome march, and a big "Hurrah for Flavius!" went up all around the plaza. There was evidently great joy in heaven for his arrival. The poster had said that all those wishing to celebrate his arrival were invited to the reception in his honor.

This didn't set well with the opposition crowd, and complaints were heard that nothing like that had taken place when they arrived, and they wondered why. But they had other problems, big complications, to consider. They felt it was their duty to maintain a pure environment free from all dissenters and heretics. They were visibly worried.

The one seeming to be in charge began speaking to those around. "How in heaven's name did he get in here? He must have bought his way in. He never came to our church, never gave any money to its support, and on Sundays he always went fishing or watched some sporting event. At least we kept ourselves pure. Flavius was a renegade and a-good-for-nothing rascal; and if my spiritual insight tells me anything, it's that he is probably the same now as he has always been. So we shouldn't expect any change with that guy. If only he could have believed the way we did, attended our prayer meetings and all the functions in our church! If he could only have been like us!"

"Why do you call him a renegade and rascal? He must have done something very evil, is that right?" someone near him asked.

"He wasn't like us! And that is bad enough. Besides, the teachings of our denomination clearly indicate that to get into Heaven you have to be orthodox like us. Sometimes I think that God should declare Himself an orthodox. That, of course, would be the only civilized thing to do. What else could He be?"

The one who had taken charge of this group, Michael O. B. Noxious, looked over his "congregation" and with a stern face continued his monologue: "We prayed hard that the Good Lord would bless our church, and give us favor above everybody else. As you know, we had to defend our faith, for we were always right, and the others were dead wrong. Now we are faced with a dilemma. Flavius, who paid no attention to anything we taught and preached, is now in the same place we are. If we allow this to go on, he'll soon contaminate everything. Heaven will lose its reputation, and then," he paused to add some drama to his outrage "Heaven wouldn't be Heaven!"

"But for now the immediate need is to find out from the officials how Flavius can be sent to the other place, where he really belongs. You have all heard about that locale; you know, where they could use an air-conditioning system. We'll just have to find out how he got here. I'll convince those in charge not to allow Flavius to stay here after all, and that shouldn't be very difficult." With that Michael instructed the crowd to wait for him while he petitioned the admissions official with his already well-prepared convincing statements.

Michael was a tall, slender man, a died-in-the-wool orthodox, who all his religious life on Earth had preached hell, fire and brimstone. He had graduated from a seminary, and for a while had taught theology there--his own theology of course--before deciding to accept a pastorate in a small church. His enthusiasm and demanding loud voice had brought many new members to the congregation. Over a ten year period he had built the membership from a mere 35 to over 1500!! He was building a congregation after his own image, and when he died he was sure to go to Heaven.

Heaven for him was a place where God was present and all those who didn't believe like himself would not be permitted to enter. Michael was sure that's the way it had to work out. That was rule no 7, paragraph 4, on page 34 of "Rules, Humility and Misgivings," treasured by the whole congregation. Michael had written it all by himself, by inspiration of course, and was very proud of that volume. In addition, he had written and published 22 books on the righteous life according to Michael O. B. Noxious.

He approached someone wearing a sizable badge made from pure silver; it hung from a gold chain that he wore around his neck. The word "OFFICIAL" was inscribed on the badge for all to see. Michael asked him quite directly why a scoundrel like Flavius Flatonia was allowed to enter this sacred place.

"Oh yes, saint Flatonia is allowed by the highest authority to enter here. There isn't anything you or anybody else can do about that."

"I will not be seen in the company of this, this--. So now he is a saint, eh? There is no justice at all!"

"But there is," the official corrected Michael. "You didn't know that although Flavius never professed the same faith as so many of you did, nevertheless he believed in all aspects of God. He served God in many ways: when he cared for the sick, when he paid the hospital bills for children whose parents were poor, distributed food to the hungry, and yes, when he went fishing or watched some sporting events. But he never went alone. There were always children in his company.

"He did all that while you and your congregation were feeling very safe, secure and righteous. Oh yes, you and your people did a great deal of work in and around your community, that's true; but with what kind of attitudes? Self righteousness and haughty pride show strongly in your aura. Just examine yourself honestly and the truth will come to light. You need to know that Flavius has faith in God, and has served HIM with a true heart.

"By the way, did you know that Judas, the one who betrayed Jesus, has been here for some time? From observing your attitude I doubt that you'd be delighted to hear such a thing, but that's the way it is. You should also know that many souls here have complained about the presence of people like YOU. They too have said that with your kind here this can't be heaven. So you see it goes both ways."

"But that can't be," Michael exclaimed with astonishment. "And Judas wasn't a Christian," Michael loudly protested. "And I have believed that only Christians are allowed in Heaven. I can't be wrong! Are you sure you know what you're talking about?"

"Let me assure you," the official answered, "I know quite well what I'm talking about. I want to remind you that Judas was one of the 12 disciples chosen by Jesus.

"You need to recognize that to enter Heaven there is no requirement that one has to be a member of a particular denomination/church, synagogue, or mosque or temple. This place is for God's creation.

"Furthermore, there is also room in Heaven for those who come from other solar systems far removed from your own 'Milky Way.' I hope you understand that."

"I don't and I won't understand that. But what about Hell, then?" Michael countered.

"It says in your Bible," the official responded, "a book you claim to be very familiar with, that death and Hell gave up the dead, and also that death and Hell were cast into the lake of fire. In another place it says that God is a consuming fire. While you're here you might want to think about what that could mean."

Michael stood there astonished, with his mouth wide open and his eyes as big as saucers. He started to protest. "But this can't be possible! I have it on good authority that--"

"Coming back to Flavius," the official interrupted, "if you would check your appointment calendar, you will readily see that you are scheduled to attend his classes as soon as he is ready for his first session. I'm sure you'll love the arrangements we have made for you and your followers. Do you have anything further to add?"

"Yes. It isn't morally right to allow Flavius in here. His presence will contaminate this place. Besides, we, meaning those of my followers, have been faithful and served God for many years. If people like Flavius were allowed in Heaven, tell me what good is it to have believed like we did only to find that unbelievers are also here? I am sure a great mistake has been made. Don't you agree?"

"If Heaven becomes contaminated that's really not your problem, and from our point of view it isn't a problem at all. After all, Flavius served God many years also. Those who didn't believe like you and your followers have much to learn, even as you do. All people are allowed here, they are all God's people, so that they can learn and get on with the issues of life. Where else could they learn? They need love, caring and consideration, and they will receive that here. I'm sure you've heard that you should love your neighbor as yourself?"

"Of course I have. I have preached and taught on that subject for many years. In fact, I have written a book and numerous articles on that topic. I'm not totally without any knowledge." Michael had become very defensive now.

"Yes, we know all this and much, much more about you than you realize. But the decision is final. Flavius has entered Heaven. Any further questions?"

Michael had nothing more to say; he had asked too many questions already, and he didn't like any of the answers. They were all against his long established doctrine. His body trembling with anger, he returned to his followers.

"Flavius will be here," Michael reported to them with a nervous voice. "There isn't anything we can do about it. And if he is allowed here, there is no telling who else might enter," he mournfully complained. A cry of agony was heard from the members of the group.

"But I thought that Heaven was a place where everybody agreed about their faith, like us. But with this fellow here, and probably others like him, this won't be Heaven at all," one of the members complained.

"That's right," Michael responded, "but for the time being we'll have to accept the order from the official about this. He claims that Flavius loved God and served Him for many years--only not in a church. But worse than that, we're all scheduled to attend a class with Flavius as the teacher."

A spectator standing near by chuckled. "You know," he remarked to his companion, "Michael has been in six classes already, but each time he disrupted them so much that the teacher had to tell him to leave.

"In each case he told the teacher that error was being taught, and that he, Michael, would be glad to teach to the class what was right and true. Michael was always quick to tell them that he had all the truth there was. Every time he did that, he regularly tried to take over the class, but had, fortunately, failed. Nevertheless, he just might try again. Well, there is usually one in every crowd. It seems to me that we have an excess here of characters like that. I just don't understand why he doesn't learn."

I had witnessed these events with amazement at the attitudes I had seen in Michael and his followers. I thought that everything in Heaven would be so peaceful and harmonious that there would never be any behavior like that. I looked at Asne and Jacob with this question on my mind: "How could anything like that take place here?"

"Remember," Asne said, "they carry their human-like traits here just as they had on Earth. As a tree falls, so it lies. It takes a long time before a soul begins to mature.

"When a soul first arrives here, it is overcome with all the love it feels. But as it adjusts to this environment, the traits expressed on Earth emerge from time to time. It is more difficult to unlearn the wrong things than to learn new truths.

"That's why it is so difficult for those who insist on returning to Earth right away. They keep making the same mistakes over and over again. Jacob and I have decided to stay here for as long as we can because we are tired of making the same mistakes. Perhaps after we have grown a little, we can return to Earth and make new mistakes instead of the old ones. Make no mistake about it!" she finished her statement with a twinkle in her eye.

It was time to choose our next stop. With only a one day pass it was up to me to decide where I wanted to go. After a little discussion among the three of us, we agreed to visit Flavius' class if we could get in. The class would probably be filled to capacity, but it was worth a try. I couldn't resist the curiosity to see how O. B. Noxious would handle himself in a classroom situation.

A clerk in a nearby information booth gave us directions to that class. I received several pages of data which told me much about the teacher, Flavius Flatonia, and what he would teach.

To the amazement of all three of us, we discovered that Flavius had been a professor of history, ancient and current. He had written volumes on the cultural development of civilizations, had lectured throughout the world, and had also been an advisor to many governments. All of his books were available at the lending library, a division of The Great Library. His special interest, it was noted, was to promote peace, understanding and good will among all people. He didn't tolerate intolerance and was often quite vocal about it. But he meant well. He was a **humanitarian**; although he seldom, if ever, attended church, he had a strong faith in God. Without a doubt this puzzled most church-going believers. He had read much and was very knowledgeable about every religious belief system on the Earth.

In addition, he was also a lecturer on dreams, having studied the collective works of Carl Jung, Sigmund Freud and many others. He also had a sparkling curiosity about mythology, traditions and superstitions.

During his last incarnation he had gravitated towards people who could stimulate his thinking and imagination. In that pursuit he had become greatly interested in music and color therapy. He was most curious about how these two elements affected the well being of the physical, spiritual, emotional and intellectual bodies. He had read about some experiments with music and color therapy that had taken place, and the reported conclusions were very startling.

People, it was reported, had actually been healed from whatever ailed them, which to Flavius was hard to believe. How could simple elements like music and color be so effective in healing when traditional means had often failed? He questioned this to a high degree and had written it off as a hoax when he witnessed a session for himself. This alone convinced him that there was more to this kind of therapy than met the eye and mind. It was non-invasive and was very pleasant to the client, and so inexpensive that everybody could afford it.

He thought that this could possibly be the next major breakthrough in the field of alternative medicine. After all, it had been used in healing animals and plants, so why not the human species? He was careful not to tell his associates about his new discovery, for he knew how dogmatic and inflexible they were. He didn't want to take any undue risks with his career, which up to this point had been irreproachable. So he kept this knowledge to himself, even though his library contained a number of articles and books on the subject.

Up to his last days he maintained an interest in just about every facet of human endeavor, and encouraged many of his contemporaries to reach beyond their own self-imposed limitations.

"You will notice," the clerk started to explain, "that there is a map on the wall to your right that gives a description of all the courses given here. The one Flavius Flatonia teaches is an introductory session, later he will also be teaching several advanced courses. You may know already that it is much more difficult to teach an introductory course than an advanced one. The groundwork, the foundation, is laid there, and upon that foundation the students will build additional knowledge. If the foundation is faulty, what is built on it may also be faulty. Therefore, great skill and knowledge, discipline and experience, are required to teach any introductory course. But you knew that already didn't you?"

I had known about this for a long time, so I nodded yes.

"This large map," and the clerk pointed to it, "gives you an overview of the entire complex available to you at this time. Look at these seven large buildings!" She appeared so proud, as if she had built them herself without any help from others.

"The School of Living is located in these buildings. This school, a progressive one, teaches the students how to live in a world that is hostile to peace and cooperation. The course work does not teach how to improve technology, but how to improve the individual thinking patterns. For as you know, as a person thinks, so *is* that person in every respect, and so *is* the world which that person creates.. You will hear more about that if you attend any of the classes in this school.

"You will notice," the clerk continued, "that these seven buildings are arranged in the shape of the Ankh, an ancient symbol for life. You will see this particular symbol repeated many times in the architecture, and in the gardens and furnishings in this complex. Learning to live is taken very seriously here, and we hope that all the students who go through these courses may take with them something of substance when they return to Earth. When people learn to live, then perhaps there can be peace in the Universe. Planet Earth is being watched very carefully, not only by us but also by other planetary systems that are so far advanced they would astound you.

"The foundation teaching of the School of Living is that it uses the seven chakras, or spiritual centers, as the springboard for the instruction and course work. Thus the student will understand to a better degree what each of the chakras mean and how to use them, not only physiologically, but more importantly, spiritually. If time allows, and as you listen to the lectures, and hopefully participate in the question and answer sessions, you will become better acquainted with the subject of learning to live.

"However, I do suggest that you first attend the introductory session of Flavius Flatonia. It promises to be a very lively class, to say the least. According to the roster, a Michael O.B. Noxious with a number of his followers has been admitted to the same class. You might want to be careful not to get too emotionally involved in the discussion that follows that lecture.

"At the end of the first session with Flavius, you are free to attend one of the classes at the School of Living, if you wish. Good luck and have fun."

She told us where the class with Flavius would be held, and pointed in the direction of the building.

Chapter 6

Heavenly Discussions

The class was filled to capacity. All 50,000 seats were occupied except for three way in the back. "Just as I thought. Too bad we didn't get here earlier. I sure would have liked to have a seat closer to the front. Oh well, I'll try to make the best of a not so good situation," I sounded off to Asne and Jacob. I showed my visitor's pass to the attendant at the door.

"Well, you finally arrived," he remarked to us. "We saw from the computer printout that you were coming, so we saved seats for you and your sister and brother. No need to rush; the class can't start until the teacher, Flavius Flatonia, arrives. But you are just in time. Did you enjoy your visit to The Great Library?" While talking he motioned to an usher, and we were taken to the last three seats in the back.

"Glad you are here!" The usher greeted us cheerfully. "Hope you enjoy the class." With that we were given a program that explained the purpose of the class and what the teacher would cover. The program further said that the session would take about five years, but visitors could leave any time they so desired.

I had a lively interest in this class, and wanted to know everything about it. I felt I should get acquainted with the course work so that I could have a good idea of what was to be taught, what its development was, and see if I could learn it all in the short time I would be there. Looking at Asne and Jacob, who were busy conversing with those next to them, I bent close to the seat in front of me. Tapping the person on the shoulder, I said, "I'm from planet Earth. Where do you come from?"

"I'm from the Pleiades, a wonderful place to be. As you may know, the Pleiades is a long distance from planet Earth, about 10 million light years, as you count time and distance. We have a long life span there, and for that reason we have the opportunity to contribute a great deal in just one lifetime. I hope that you will have a chance to visit us sometime."

"I'd like to. Tell me more about the Pleiades. It sounds like a stimulating place to live."

"It is! If you ever get there I'll show you around. You'll have a wonderful time experiencing something quite different. Oh, I see you are a visitor here."

Looking for the expiration date on the pass, he remarked, "Well you are here for a whole day! That's more time than most visitors are allowed here. Do you know anybody special? Have you achieved something great? Are you the one who--?"

"Attention! The class will start in exactly two minutes. You will all want to pay close attention when Dr. Flavius Flatonia starts his lecture. If you have any questions for him, please keep them in your mind; or better, write them down on a piece of paper, and ask them during the time provided for questions. All queries will be answered, provided there are explanations available, no matter how long it takes. Our last session, which was given by another teacher, lasted close to five years, Earth time, with the question and answer period taking about four years to complete."

The one making the announcement, a tall, stately woman, paused and looked around to determine if everything was set for the start of the class. With a smile she turned to the class, "Now, let us welcome the eminent Dr. Flavius Flatonia."

Amidst cheers of welcome and approval the applause was deafening. It lasted a long time, and all the while Dr. Flatonia acknowledged the welcome with repeated words of "Thank you, thank you; good to be back. Nice to see you all." He waved his hand and smiled to everybody. He was quite a handsome man, rather tall, and somewhat overweight, as is true with so many of us as we get older. He was in his late 70's, with a full head of hair that had turned to an appealing white. His steel gray eyes, framed by a pair of bushy eyebrows, caught every detail of this welcome. Needless to say he was very pleased. He really hadn't expected such a demonstrative welcome, but he took it all in.

He remembered he had been in other classrooms many times before, so this was nothing new to him. Nevertheless, he enjoyed the spontaneous outburst of applause from the crowd. This was his moment of glory. He now had to go on with the lesson, which he knew would take a great deal of energy from him. For now, this was his first assignment since arriving here.

As he stood on the podium, he remembered how many difficult assignments he had accepted when he was on Earth, and how he faced them with some degree of awe because he didn't know what the results would be. Very often he just had to take a chance, trusting that his experience and knowledge could be combined with a teaspoon of creativity and a pinch of intuition. It always worked. He believed that this present assignment would be a challenge to him too, and he considered it a wonderful way for him to learn.

He motioned to the class to be silent. Looking over the auditorium he noticed people from every country in the world, as well as a number of students from places beyond the Milky Way solar system. He recognized their unique skin color, the slender faces and big, meaningful eyes. "Well" he thought "a great part of the Universe is represented here. This should be very interesting."

"I want to welcome you to my class!" Flavius began. "You'll find that we're very informal, and I hope you'll call me Flavius instead of Dr. Flatonia. Because of a previously arranged engagement, this session will be very short, no more than five years in Earth time. In addition to my lecture there will be a number of workshops, which will be led by my able assistant Aristotle Schwartz. His brother, Summer Schwartz, is in charge of security in this school. Prior to their arrival here, they had lived in the southern part of the United States of America. They are interesting people, so you'll want to introduce yourselves to them when it is convenient. I see that we have three visitors in the back row. It is a privilege to have you with us.

"Now, there may be some members of this class who will not agree with everything in my lecture. I'm sure you're not going to leave, stomping your feet and slamming the door behind you as a way of expressing your disapproval." He paused and looked around the huge auditorium. "I have a list," he said, "of names of individuals who have established a (pardon the expression) reputation for trying to disrupt the class with the intent of taking it over. At the top of my list is a Michael O. B. Noxious who is seated in the front row center. Will you please stand Michael?"

Michael stood, expecting some sort of recognition or approval from the audience, but it was all very quiet. Flavius thanked him, saying, "You may be seated."

Flavius continued, "I want everyone in the class to know that any disruption will be cause for expulsion. We're all here to learn, and we want a pleasant environment for this.

"To begin with, there are eight important subjects that I will bring out in my lecture, but each subject will be dealt with in greater detail when you attend the School of Living. This class will give you an overview of some of the subjects that are offered.

"Subject number one: What do we mean by learning how to live? Or simply put, how are we to live?"

Michael sprang to his feet and started to answer it. Flavius stopped him, and explained that this was a question directed to the class for the purpose of pondering for the moment. Disappointed, Michael slumped down in his seat

"As you should know, life was always meant to be an experience to be lived, not a problem to be solved. Let us first deal with life on planet Earth. The way many of you have lived on Earth has been, for the most part, a puzzle to which you have found no answers, only consternation. You have created for yourselves an environment that is filled with frustration, anger, resentment and unforgiving attitudes. In the School of Living more will be revealed to you about the treasures found within the spirit of forgiveness.

"Many have blamed others for their own mistakes, and have kept on making the same mistakes over and over again, life after life. In this way you have managed to make your own hell on Earth. To overcome this pattern you do not stop this kind of behavior by trying to get rid of it. If you do, you are only getting rid of part of yourself. Instead, seek transformation from within and become a new and different person so that your behavior will change.

"Here are some brief examples: If you have a pattern of stealing in your life, inwardly transform the energy used for that, and find ways to give. If you have a pattern of lying, transform that energy into telling the truth.

"Along each step of the way you can actually rebuild your own soul structure, and no longer be subject to negative patterns. All this will, of course, take time, but with a little patience and proper motives this too can be accomplished.

"Subject number two deals with motives. This is often a deceptive factor in the lives of many, because motives aren't always recognized or known. Not because they are elusive, but because many haven't understood the importance of honest motives carried out with integrity. Motives, which are the driving force behind every decision and action in everyone's life, are more important than most souls understand. They can be like a compass that may also show you when you are on the right or wrong path.

"Subject number three: this is an important aspect to consider in our introductory class; namely, why do you believe what you believe? I am not addressing myself to any particular group, but to all belief systems. The question is, why do you believe the dogmas, creeds, teachings, traditions, and anything else you may think of and have been practicing when you lived on Earth.

"I think it would be timely to invite some questions on the first three topics mentioned to stimulate your thinking. There are five more topics to consider, but these I will only mention toward the end of this session. More will be said about these, and hopefully in greater detail, when you attend the School of Living. Just remember, don't come to any quick conclusions. After you have gone through all the courses in the School of Living, you may very well have changed your mind a dozen or more times. So be patient with yourselves. Now, any questions at all?"

All over the auditorium hands were seen held up high, each one begging for recognition. Flavius looked out over the class and pointed in the direction towards the back. I also had my hand up, and I thought I was invited to ask a question. But before I could get to my feet, the person right in front of me stood up to ask a question.

"Yes, the gentleman from the Pleiades," Flavius acknowledged. "Let's hear his question. Go on," and he motioned to him.

"My question is, why is it so important to believe? Where I come from we have no definite belief system as so many here call it. Does it make you feel better, live better, make a better impression on others if you believe in something? The reason I am asking these questions is that we have faith in nothing and yet faith in everything. Does that make sense to you? Whether or not it makes sense to you, I'd like to have your comments. Thank you for allowing me to express myself."

Michael jettisoned to his feet and spoke out loud. Very loud, and very clear. "It is very important that you have faith in something that has been proven, and that many people believe in. Let me explain so that you may know what real faith is."

He approached the podium in order to be seen as well as heard by the many onlookers. He hadn't given up his plan to take over the class, and teach the students according to his own belief. Somebody had to teach THE TRUTH, he thought, for as he believed, he knew it all. With determined and quick steps he made his approach, and was sure that no one dared stop him this time. He had tried in six previous classes, and had been unsuccessful. However, now he had a plan. His followers, and there were many of them in the audience, he thought would support him. According to his plan they would insist that he, Michael, be the teacher, and would not be satisfied until this was accomplished.

To his surprise and shock there was nobody to support him. He looked out over the audience and found no one rising to his or her feet demanding that Michael take over the class. Michael's face clearly questioned this unexpected outcome, and his expression suggested an explanation was in order. He glanced at Flavius.

"I have taken measures," Flavius spoke with a clear, crisp voice, "to prevent a hostile takeover. I'll have chief of security, Mr. Summer Schwartz, explain."

Summer Schwartz stepped forward and with an authoritative voice clarified the situation. "We had known for some time," he said, "that a situation like this would take place, for it has happened before. So we redirected all the followers of Michael to another section of this building, split them up in small groups, and then assigned them to different introductory classes. We don't want a repetition of what took place before. Incidents like these would give us a bad reputation, and the top management would take a dim view of such disturbances. There are disciplines and certain rules to be followed here. I am sure that you all understand. Thank you for your attention. Dr. Flavius Flatonia will continue with the question and answer period."

Sheepishly Michael returned to his seat.

"To answer the question about believing and faith," Flavius began, "it is very important to keep in mind that your behavior is more important than what you claim is your faith and whatever belief system you say you hold to in a life experience. It is how you live, not what you say or express in words, that tells in a most descriptive way what you truly believe. The old saying 'your actions speak louder than your words' is very appropriate for this matter. You may read volume upon volume of the finest literature you can find; you may listen to the finest orators, like Cicero, Plato, and Churchill; and you may be inspired to believe what others have related in the minutest detail. But if what you say you believe doesn't match with the way you live, you need to examine yourself and your belief.

"Which brings me back to subject number three: why do you believe what you believe? Because somebody told you? Or because you have convictions? You should know that there is a big difference between these two. Yes, you can develop convictions after you have listened to someone or read certain materials. Yet to develop your faith on the basis of what others have told you and nothing else, without going any further, will lead to disaster and frustrations and disappointments. I'm sure many of you have experienced this while on Earth, as well as those of you who have come from many other planets and solar systems.

"No matter how you look at it, it is essential to remember that there is only one Truth, but people have called that Truth by many, many names. For as you might know, truth comes in many forms and many packages, which goes only to show that..." Here he was interrupted.

"Sir, if there is only one Truth, why then is there so much fighting and disagreement among so many groups on Earth? I just came from there, and I also heard over and over again that unless two agree, they can't walk together. Can you shed some light on this?" The question had come from a lady who evidently was sincere about knowing the truth about the Truth.

"I shall be happy to set you right," Michael again called out loud and clear, as he quickly got up from his seat and approached the microphone on the podium. But one look from Flavius convinced him that this wasn't a very good idea. So he slowly and reluctantly returned to his seat and sat down. He knew that if he kept on interfering like this, he no doubt would be asked to leave, placed in quarantine and not allowed to return to the class for another ten years. "f only I had my people with me, things would be easier, he thought Perhaps a more opportune time will come later."

He noticed the discouraging eye of disapproval from Flavius which told him that there wouldn't be an opportune time, now or later. Don't even think about it!

"Now, let's come back to the question from the lady," Flavius began. "Namely, if there is only one truth, why is there so much fighting and disagreement among so many people about it?

"That question needs to be repeated, because if there is only one truth, why do people disagree so much over the same issue? Let me see if I can illustrate this with a story." He stood there in deep thought for a moment trying to find the right illustration that would bring the point home, not only to the one who asked the question but to everybody in the auditorium.

With measured words and without looking at the audience, being still in deep thought, as if in a trance, he began in a quiet voice, one that demanded attention.

"It's like the anecdote about a group of people observing how a column of light, passing through a many-faceted crystal, projects brilliant colors. As each one looks at the facet nearest him or her, each sees a slightly different color or hue. Some observe a brilliant blue, others a green. Still others insist the color is red.

"Those who see nearly the same color become friends and start an organization 'For the Preservation of the True Color.' For fear of being contaminated, they refuse to communicate with those who see different colors.

"Quickly more organizations are formed, one for every major color transmitted through the facets of the crystal.

"Each group believes the others have erred. Books are written about the errors of the many other groups. Conferences are held to warn their followers to stay away from the inaccuracies of other groups, lest they become contaminated and end up in the place that is in dire need of air conditioning. This would be very funny and ridiculous if it weren't so serious.

"Obviously, they are all correct in their first perception. Each see a different color of light depending upon which facet of the crystal they view.

Each believes that everyone else should see their color, when actually each facet exhibits its own color.

"You surely already know that truth is like a multifaceted diamond, with each facet representing a different aspect of truth or religious philosophy. Yet each facet is just a part of the same truth, only perceived from a different perspective.

Flavius continued on: "Many aspects of religious practices and beliefs of others have been questioned by those who claim to have the only truth. But truth comes in many different colors, and each color is part of the whole.

"Consider for a moment astrology as one of the facets. Although there are always those who warn against its use, we on this level know that God gave astrology to the people for a tool to use as a means for guidance. As you may realize, they were instructed that the stars in the sky had been placed there for signs and seasons. God placed a principle of guidance before the people. It was their responsibility to find the proper use of it.

"Truth, as you will learn while you are here, is called by many names. Some call truth God, others Jehovah, or Allah or Buddha or The Great Spirit. Whatever name is attached to truth, it is of the same fabric. It is important to know that all truth cannot be found in any single person, group or community. For God decided millions of years ago to plant a little truth in each individual. So if anyone desires to know more truth, it becomes necessary to learn from each other, and to try to apply to one's life what principles are discovered.

"As you can imagine, it requires cooperation from all parties involved in such a process, and of course some patience. Nevertheless, if we all try, we can learn from everyone. You will want to use discernment to differentiate between what is only dogma, rules and regulations that humanity tends to claim as truth, and what is actually truth.

"This brings me to the second part of your question: how can two walk together unless they agree? This, of course, is all very fundamental, and simple to understand. It doesn't mean what you think, or have been taught it means. Let me explain." He quickly glanced over to Michael to make sure he wasn't getting ready for another "hostile" takeover of the class. But for some mysterious and unexplained reason Michael had become very docile, even friendly in his facial expressions, if one dared go that far in hoping for a change in his attitude.

"The agreement is, of course," Flavius went on, "to WALK together. Whether it is in daily life, on the path of adventure, or in the field of science or spirituality, or whatever. The answer is very simple. To agree to walk together, to support one another even if you don't follow the same religion, is what is actually meant with this statement. Sometimes people have to agree even to disagree, though amiably, if they are to walk together. There has to be a consistency in attitude and behavior. So you see, those who walk together have to agree to do so, which means that you will cooperate and work together. When you analyze it a little closer, and look beyond the prejudice and fear, you'll stumble upon the obvious. Are there any other questions?"

Before anything could be said, a strong, loud voice broke in. It was Michael O.B. Noxious making himself heard-- again. "This is sheer blasphemy and an abomination, and I'll have nothing more to do with such erroneous teaching." Michael couldn't stand it any longer. "There isn't one shred of truth to what you have said, and I shall see to it that you are replaced with someone who knows the truth and can teach it as such." He stood up and walked out very fast, all the while stomping his feet heavily on the floor for all to hear. When he went through the door, he slammed it, very hard. His final sign of disapproval.

With a glint of humor in his eyes Flavius made a matter-of-fact comment for all to hear: "Well, everybody brings joy, some by coming, others by leaving. Seriously speaking, keep Michael in your prayers that some day he will learn to learn, that he may eventually come into the process of maturing. Now, are there any more questions before we go on?"

In the middle of the auditorium a hesitating hand was raised. Flavius beckoned to the person to state the question. Slowly, as if each movement had been rehearsed, he stood quietly to his feet, looked to Flavius and started to form his question.

"I have been listening to your introductory lecture with great interest, and the questions directed to you have made me wonder about one facet of all the speculations and questioning which I feel is circulating in the minds of many who are present here, including mine. As it has been asked before, and still continues to be posed to many sages, I feel I must direct this question to you, as well. However, let me remind you that over a period of many, many ages I have asked the same question. I even uttered it at one important historical event, and I waited for the answer, an answer I hoped would be the correct reply.

"But to my disappointment there was no answer forthcoming. The sages gave forth no utterances of wisdom; the religious people had no solution; neither did the philosophers and educators. And as I mentioned earlier, this goes back many, many ages, from the height of Atlantis, the Golden age of Egypt, the Renaissance period, and the Age of the Great Awakening.

"For sure, there have been intellectual discourses that were nothing more than analytical calisthenics, religious dogmas that were nothing more than a pious maze of philosophical statements that left the listener spellbound but not much wiser."

Laughter, in a quiet and dignified manner, was heard all over the auditorium.

"So here is my question: What is Truth?" As quietly as he had stood up he started to sit down. He was stopped by Flavius, who in a kind and concerned voice asked him to remain standing.

"I appreciate your statement and the question, and I am sure the same appreciation is expressed by all these present. Before you sit down, please tell us your name."

The man hesitated. He felt that he didn't want to influence what answer Flavius would develop, so he thought it would be the better part of wisdom not to reveal his name. By now he had everybody's attention; they were all looking at him, some sitting at the edge of their seats waiting for him to speak.

He was a very tall man, slender, with blond hair and bright blue eyes. His facial features, which were quite distinct, could make him out to be either Grecian or Roman. When he spoke he expressed himself with dignity and kindness. Every word, like a ray of sunshine, showed its sincerity and gentleness. He never hesitated while he had the floor, as if he had practiced his little speech for many years; or else perhaps he had made the same statement many times over a period of many ages.

"My name is," and he paused; not for dramatic purposes, but because he really didn't want to give it.

"You promise not to make light of me if I tell you?" the stately figure continued cautiously. "You see, at one time I was confronted with The Truth, and I still asked, 'What is Truth'? My name--is--Pontius Pilate." His voice had dropped to a whisper, but the acoustics in the auditorium were excellent, and every member of the class heard his name.

The audience was very silent. They could all perceive his longing to know the Truth, for they all felt the same. Then suddenly they broke into an astounding applause and got to their feet and continued their applause. This went on for some time until Flavius was able to quiet them, thanking them all for their response and understanding.

"This is a most challenging question and it certainly deserves an answer that will measure up to it. Recognizing the response you gave Pontius Pilate tells me that many of you certainly do have the same question.. Perhaps in many lifetimes, and through many different and painful encounters, we all have met Truth. Not having understood and perhaps not believed, we have questioned that to which we have been exposed. Or our hearts have believed and even understood, yet our intellect has said something different. That internal conflict has often blocked the resolution. We have heard the question; dear friends, let's now search for the answer."

Chapter 7

Precarious Truth?

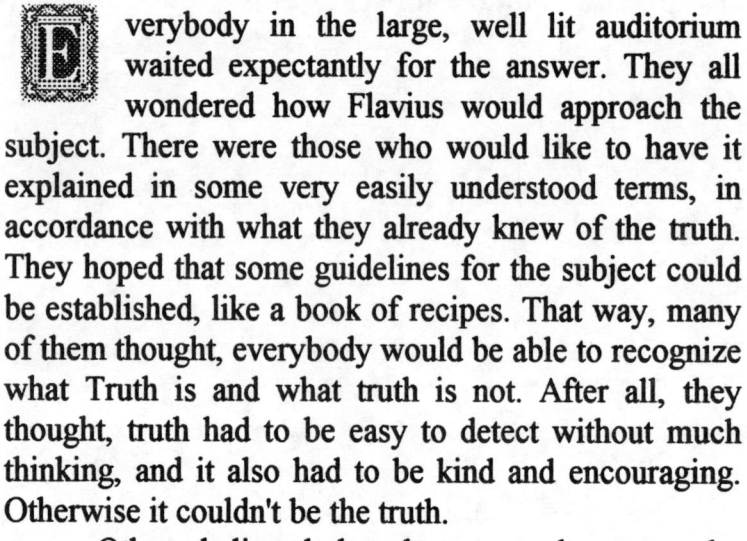

Everybody in the large, well lit auditorium waited expectantly for the answer. They all wondered how Flavius would approach the subject. There were those who would like to have it explained in some very easily understood terms, in accordance with what they already knew of the truth. They hoped that some guidelines for the subject could be established, like a book of recipes. That way, many of them thought, everybody would be able to recognize what Truth is and what truth is not. After all, they thought, truth had to be easy to detect without much thinking, and it also had to be kind and encouraging. Otherwise it couldn't be the truth.

Others believed that they were the ones who had the truth and they thought that they had it all. According to that group this was a black and white turf. This topic didn't fit into any gray areas, so they thought. It was clear as well water to them that nobody should argue about the truth, for it had been cast in concrete eons ago. It was unchangeable. Truth was truth. In addition, it had to fit into the format of the majority of believers, and of course in their opinion there had to be agreement. It was obvious that they hadn't heard a word of what Flavius had said about agreement.

Still others believed that truth is wherever you find it, but you might have to look for it. Then there were those who were convinced that truth would seek them out, without any effort on their part. That by some mystical process of osmosis they would know the truth.

While all of this was going on in the minds of many people, I looked at Jacob and remembered how he had been searching for truth while living in the midst of a stagnant community. I remembered how, in his search for truth and spiritual stimulation, he had deliberately isolated himself from his relatives and turned to people who could challenge him in his search.

It had been difficult for him, always being questioned by his relatives as to why he had withdrawn from their social and religious circles. Each time he was confronted, he would come up with some excuse of just being too busy. Yet when I took Doris to Norway to meet my family Jacob relaxed his isolation and attended all the social functions that were given in our honor. Privately over coffee at the hotel he told us that from what he could perceive, their mentality and outlook hadn't changed at all over all the years he had lived in Trondheim. He told us that he was seeking for something that would challenge and stimulate him in his daily life, something from which he could grow spiritually. It had been a lonely life for him, which showed in his face, particularly in his eyes.

He chose to be lonely rather than to congregate with people who had no desire for seeking truth and greater meaning to life. People who just gossiped bored him. During our visit to Trondheim Jacob always ended up joining the group of relatives talking with us. He knew that we tried to guide the conversation to matters of substance and spiritual growth.

Before Flavius began his explanation about truth, I turned to Jacob and asked him how he looked at truth and how he perceived it.

"It is so much easier to understand truth when you are with souls who are searching for truth and have that desire in common," he replied. "At first, after I arrived here, the truth I heard was a little difficult for me to understand, even though it was delivered to me with such love and caring. This I had seldom experienced when I was on planet Earth. But after a short while I realized that truth and love go hand in hand. Truth without love is an intellectual exercise and doesn't go very far. Shhh! the lecture is about to begin."

Flavius saw the many different and controversial thought forms developing, and he knew everyone wanted to be right. This was consistent with most of his previous classes on this subject. It appeared to him that there was much disagreement among them, and no one had any desire to give in to the other. Afterall, this concept is what they had been taught, and what some had been teaching. So, they all thought, they must be right and the others wrong. Flavius knew this was a very sensitive subject, requiring diplomacy, insight and flexibility on his part to bring to the class new concepts from which they could learn. Flavius knew quite well that he didn't have all the answers, especially to this particular and important question. This certainly was a fundamental question upon which all issues of life rest.

It would be very easy to lay before them some dogmas and rules and tell the listeners that that's the way it was, is, and will be. But would that be the highest approach, and would it bring the point home to each person, meeting his and her needs right where they are? Flavius continued to observe and perceive the temperament of the class. How acceptable would they be to what he would teach about Truth?

He knew, of course, that the religious flash point was very low among many seated before him, and yet he had to venture out and begin to try to explain what probably already was, and no doubt would remain, the controversial subject matter of the Universe.

"To start with," he began somewhat carefully, "let me say that truth is everywhere. This concept, of course, contradicts the more narrow beliefs of many people who over the years have heard this and even repeated it without thinking what it really means. Truth is--" and here he paused in order to get everybody's focus on what was to come. He felt he needed to call them from their separate thoughts and already made-up minds to an attitude of undivided attention.

"Yes, truth is found in the principle embodied within a concept or philosophy that is meaningful to you. However, no matter how wonderful and beautiful a statement is, and no matter how much others state that this is truth it never becomes truth to you unless you begin to live it. I may have to approach this subject in a round-about manner, so please bear with me for the time being.

"In the process of seeking for truth and in an effort to determine what is truth, people have often clothed a concept of truth in terms that are more acceptable to them, resulting in a complete disguise of that truth. Truth, when it is truth, can be tested in the crucible of the practical applications of its principles in your personal life.

"Those of you who have studied with some prominent teachers may have become spellbound by the personality and charisma of these persons. As a result, you began to repeat information from their teachings without giving much thought to their validity and truthfulness. So you fall into the trap that has existed in the Universe for ages, namely: becoming infatuated with the charismatic personality and blinded by the oratory, and deceived by the presence of the large crowds.

"This has been a great deception throughout the ages and seekers have been led to believe that because so many scholars, teachers and famous people agree on certain issues, it must be the truth, by definition. Understand something. Although experts/scholars may agree with each other, they can still be wrong.

"Having said all this, I submit to you, can truth be defined? Is truth established by merely repeating specific statements or creeds? No. Does truth depend upon its being accepted by large or small groups? No.

If truth is not accepted by the majority, is it still truth? Yes!

"The challenge of seeking truth is that you will continually come across small parts of the bigger picture that you may not like. Chances are that if you're not familiar with what you find, you won't be happy with your discovery. But then, happiness in this case is not a requirement; honesty and integrity are. Honesty and integrity with self, and the courage to go beyond that part of truth you presently hold so dear. Don't make one truth your unchanging god. Truth, like everything else in the Universe, must grow.

"Have you noticed in your own growth how your concepts of truth have developed to take in more of the whole of a certain aspect of truth? Many of you have come into one understanding of a truth and lived it for years. Then for whatever reason, greater understanding has come to you concerning it, and you have moved to a position on it that may be almost unrecognizable to the first position. Yet both were truth to you. The latter was simply an expansion of the former. That truth had grown because you have grown."

Flavius paused, determining the pulse of the audience. Had he gone too far, or not far enough? The auditorium had been bathed in deep silence. Everybody had paid close attention to every word spoken.

Now Flavius could hear the "wheels grinding" as they thought over what he had said up to now. As he looked out over the audience, some heads here and there nodded "Yes," although, at the same time there were many others who violently disagreed. He could tell they were fearful that the truth they had known for so long might not be the truth after all.

Anger had risen in their hearts. Flavius could see it. They were astounded that someone would dare to challenge the truth they had. Several were ready to fight Flavius on the issue of "What is truth?" because they thought that they had it all defined and knew quite well what it was. Flavius detected that a number of them would like to set him straight, according to their understanding of truth.

He could see that already people had gathered mentally in groups, and were making plans, big ones, to correct the speaker. It appeared that somebody besides Michael O.B. Noxious would like to take over the class.

Flavius knew that he had opened up a delicate and very controversial concept. He braced himself for an attack from the listeners, for this never failed to ignite a lively response. He knew his explanation so far hadn't set right with the crowd; he could feel it. And he was right.

The atmosphere was filled with a combustible mixture of fear and anger. He decided to give them an opportunity to express themselves.

"Before I go on, are there any questions regarding what I have presented so far?" He didn't have to wait long.

"Sir," a loud voice came from the back, a few seats over to my right. Flavius turned in the direction of the voice and recognized who it was. He motioned to him to rise and state his question.

With a little difficulty he got to his feet. From what I could tell he was short, a few inches over five feet, and well proportioned in many places. A long, full beard hid most of his face, his chest and a large part of his stomach. On his head he had a white skull cap. Over his black suit, worn to a very nice polish, he wore a long, wide, white prayer shawl. I spotted the phylacteries on his left arm, under the sleeve, and the one around his head. From the way he looked, he appeared to be a very religious man who practiced his faith very seriously.

He looked around, appearing to be quite nervous, as though this might be the first time he had faced such a large audience. He moistened his lips while getting ready to make a statement. Bringing out a large white handkerchief he wiped the perspiration from his forehead. With slow, calculating motions he wrung his hands, shifting his weight from one foot to the other, as if to apologize for his presence.

The silence over the auditorium was so piercing one could hear a thought fall.

Finally he cleared his throat, looked up at Flavius and with measured words started:

"My name is Caiaphas. I am sure many of you may know who I am. I don't actually have a question, but I'd like to make some comments. At one time I played the role of the High Priest in a performance whose outcome changed the world in many ways. I am not so sure that I played my role as well as I could have. Nevertheless, this was the 'play' I was to be in, and the role I had auditioned for prior to returning to Earth at that time. Although the aftermath of the 'play' was more extreme than I had anticipated, it brought about a significant change in many lives; including mine.

"While I had been brought up at that time in an atmosphere of traditions, rules and regulations, I was inwardly wondering if what I had been taught was the only truth. The question of truth often came into my mind, yet I seldom had much of an opportunity to give it any thought. From early childhood I was taught that at the proper time I would be given all the truth there was, and for me not to question it.

"At an early age I married Zeporah, the daughter of the High Priest, hoping eventually to inherit that position. I had friends among the Sanhedran, the high council in the Temple, consisting of the most brilliant scholars to be found for miles around. Among them were Joseph of Arimethia and a bright and aggressive young man called Saul of Tarsus. While in training for the priesthood, I would often talk with them about truth, and what part it should have in our lives. Our discussions would often revolve around how it could be discovered; was it by study, by consensus, by revelation, or from an inner knowledge?

"I soon discovered that even a simple question like that had no easy or direct answer. Saul was quick to respond that truth can be discovered only by a consensus of a body of scholars like the Sanhedran. There had to be agreement, he insisted, among all the recognized scholars, so that there could be a unified position. In addition, it was pointed out to me that traditions played a very important part in establishing truth. Saul was very insistent that rules, dogmas, precedence and established traditions must be considered in trying to understand such a difficult and complex subject.

"However, Joseph of Arimethea had a different viewpoint. Truth, he claimed, could only be understood through revelation as one studied sacred writings, and in the discussion of the same with learned scholars. Truth has to be discerned by a blend of reason and intuition; and for it to come alive its principles must be practiced in daily life. Joseph was a man of few words, but what he said always went deep into my soul.

"I also witnessed, however, the debate of the many members of the Sanhedran, and there was a constant disagreement concerning truth. So what was I to believe? I felt the best course of action for me was to follow traditions, and let truth come through that method. When I then became the High Priest, I was deeply entrenched in the customs of the time, and had already forgotten the words of Joseph of Arimethea.

"I wanted to do what was right, of course, but at the same time I also wanted to protect my status as High Priest. I believe most people in responsible positions might do the same, don't you agree?" He looked around for approval to his question, and found a number of people registering what he wanted to see.

After a short pause to collect his thoughts, he continued: "Throughout my life journeys I have been party to many events taking place on planet Earth, such as the Council of Constantinople, the French revolution and the Boxer rebellion in China, just to mention a few. But during all that time I have tried to understand what is truth. As of now I haven't come to any definite conclusion. Therefore, I am eager to hear more from you on this, if you can enlighten me on the subject." With that he sat down. Flavius observed that the whole assembly appreciated the honesty of Caiaphas.

Sitting in the back row I made a gesture to Asne and Jacob that I had a comment to make, and started to get up from my chair. I had already prepared in my mind what I was going to say, and felt very confident that I would be able to expand and clarify the whole issue.

"Don't you dare get up and open your mouth," Asne said sternly. "Listen a moment and hear what Flavius has to say."

"Would anyone else like to make any comments?" Flavius offered. He scanned the class with his piercing eyes, and wondered if anyone would accept the challenge.

Then a woman rose to her feet. She was short and slender, with the face of a young girl. Her dark hair was cut short, giving her the appearance of a young man. Even though her manner was very serious, she managed a bashful smile. The look in her dark brown eyes indicated uncertainty about the situation, yet there was a certain determination and decisiveness in the way she stood and held her head.

Her body was straight, her head held high. The audience observed the expression of courage rising in her face. She wore a long dark garment that fell to her feet, covering her entire body. She folded her hands behind her back and stood there, like a statue, looking around the crowded classroom. She smiled as she recognized a friendly face; then her smile faded to an expression of fear when she saw some of the others.

"Somebody asked earlier--I believe it was Pontius Pilate--'What is truth?'" she began, "and I myself have wondered many times about that. I've also wondered about this: when truth is known, what is to be done with it? During many lifetimes I have been through a number of experiences, some friendly, others unpleasant and painful. At the time when I had the visions, I told the authorities about it, and assured them that God was going to help me free France from the English. As some of you may know, with the approval of the king of France, I was given a small army, and we were successful in our mission.

"However, as it was, I was captured by the English, brought before the tribunal of the Inquisition and questioned by the barbaric Bishop of Beauvais, Cauchon. On trumped up charges of heresy and witchcraft, I was condemned to death and burned at the stake on May 30, 1431. I was only 19 years old."

As she was telling her story, it became quite obvious that she was reliving that entire life, short as it was. She was all smiles when recounting the victories in which she participated, and grim when she brought up her capture and death.

"I have seen the truth and know what it can do for anyone if followed and lived. What I know of the truth is that it cannot be defined either by committee, or upon agreement by scholars or the common people. I know that truth is not just to be kept in a notebook or hidden in a cookie jar. To some whom I have met, the subject of truth was only a conversation piece. It meant nothing more.

"Unless truth is allowed to change people for the good--so that there can be love and harmony--truth is too often misunderstood and misused.

"Truth is an experiment each of us has to enter into and determine for ourselves. Yet I have also learned that truth does not remain constant. It reveals more as I open up to it." After a short pause, she concluded, "I thank all of you for listening to me, and I would like to continue this subject with any who are interested." She sat down quickly, and then bounced right back up again. "I almost forgot to tell you that when I was burned at the stake I went under the name of Joan of Arc."

A voice called out loudly: "How can truth change? Truth must be constant, like a point of reference; otherwise there wouldn't be anything we could rely on. We must have a solid foundation on which to stand, something that remains the same age after age. Everybody must agree on what is truth; otherwise there would be nothing but confusion. I have found this to be so, and I cannot understand why everybody else isn't willing to see it this way. There must be agreement in the resolution of what is truth. Don't you all agree with that? And I know that's the truth of the matter. I always speak the truth as I see it."

All this came from someone in the middle of the room. He didn't identify himself, and as soon as he finished he quickly sat down, not wanting to be noticed in case there were those who disagreed. And there was a good share of those who did just that.

"Everybody knows that truth is dynamic, not static." This voice identified himself as Jonathan, a teacher from England. "All things in the universe must of necessity expand; otherwise there will be stagnation. Therefore I cannot agree with the last statement." It was a booming voice that could be heard in every part of the large auditorium.

By now there was quite a stir in the classroom, and people felt at odds with each other. They all believed that having an answer to the initial question "What is truth?" was very important. That way they might be able to navigate themselves better through troubled and uncertain situations when they once again would return to Earth...provided, of course, that they could remember this session. There were a number of people who had risen asking for permission to speak, but while each wanted Flavius' attention, something else was taking place.

Nobody had noticed it until all eyes turned on the person who had appeared in the center aisle. A groan of agony was heard from many. "How did he get back in here?" someone said. "I thought he walked out!" said another. "Why is he back? Dr. Flavius look who has returned. Please don't let him stay. He'll only cause havoc in this class." But there were others who came to his defense.

Yes Michael O.B. Noxious had forced his way back and demanded to be allowed to stay for the duration of the class. Shouting and yelling were heard from both factions. This was first-class bedlam. I observed it all with astonishment and interest. Just like on Earth, I thought. Everything seems to remain the same no matter where I go. Why can't there be some sort of understanding among people? Turning to Jacob I remarked, "I thought that being away from the influence of planet Earth people would behave more rationally, and try to learn as quickly as they could."

Jacob looked at me and said, "Think again. Remember, as a tree falls, so it lies. Growth comes only with change, and that may take some time."

Finally Flavius took control. With a powerful swing he struck a huge temple gong with his large, heavy gavel. A deep, deafening sound penetrated the whole auditorium and everybody knew it was time to keep quiet and listen to what was coming next.

"I ask the guards to evict Michael from this room and do so immediately," Flavius commanded. Two huge guards, each over seven feet tall, came down the aisle, lifted Michael from the floor as if he were a sack of feathers, and carried him out.

"I protest! This is unlawful! I'll appeal this decision!" Michael carried on. But to no avail.

Flavius was ready to bring this session to a close. But first he knew he had to try to bring a better understanding of what is truth to those assembled in the auditorium. He also felt that although many words had been spoken by several people, the right words had not been said to make the subject clear so that everybody might discern.

"I would like to try again to explain the subject of 'What is truth?'" he began. "As you know, truth comes in many different packages and forms. Truth may not always agree with your already-made-up mind. Any time you believe that you have all the truth, you may expect a surprising turn of events, tailor made to show you that you really possess only a miniscule part of it. That is the time when you will have an opportunity to relearn and start on a new path.

"You may have discovered some facet about truth, and have tried to live in accordance with your discovery. That's good! Then you may see a friend who is following a teaching that you know about, and that by your own definition is in error. You engage your friend in some lengthy discussions about what he is following, trying to persuade him to turn back before it is too late. But your friend insists that what he has discovered is truth. After some time you sever the friendship, telling him that you can no longer maintain fellowship with him as long as he persists in error. You warn him that there is nothing but trouble and pain waiting for him unless he mends his ways. So you part." Here Flavius paused to discern how the lecture was being received so far. He detected no hostility and saw no violence in the auras of those in the auditorium. He felt it was safe to continue.

"Some years later, in your continued search, you come across something new for you. Something that you hadn't allowed for. Something that you had never considered to be truth. You stop for a while, consider what you have discovered, and decide that this 'new' discovery is truth. You make it part of your life, and find that your life is also enriched by it. Later you learn that the truth you have just uncovered is what your friend discovered some years earlier.

"Then one day another friend visits you and declares that you have come into error, and that you had better leave this concept alone. This is what you had told your other friend at an earlier time: namely that he was in error, and that he had better leave it alone.

"Now, this causes you to start to think. Could it be that truth is relative, depending upon where you are on the path, and depending upon what your understanding is? Could it be that what is truth to you may be error to another? Understand that as long as you are seeking to grow you will journey through many passages.

"In that journey, as you live, practice what you know as truth, you will become aware of others who seem to you to be practicing error, for it is different from your truth. Yet, as you grow in your truth, what you previously saw as error may begin to open up to you as truth after all. Your understanding has broadened because of your growth.

"As you journey in truth this experience of recognizing as truth what you at one time saw as error happens to you, time and time again, until you arrive at the point where you will admit that you don't have all the truth after all and that you don't understand everything either. That type of understanding cannot come by analysis. You will come to realize that truth can grow in you as long as you continue to live by the truth you have, while remaining open and daring enough to venture into the unknown.

"Although you may consider yourself to be living in your truth, many others are living in their truth as well, even if it doesn't correspond with what you consider the truth to be. So in conclusion, what is truth? Truth is a series of principles by which you may live your life. These principles may be used as a foundation on which to base your behavior; they may be used as a guideline for decisions and for setting goals and determining motives.

"Let's use the illustration of the many-faceted diamond again. In this example let's say that the diamond is all truth. Consider each facet as a facet of that truth. Now, each one of you may see only one facet at first. Whichever facet you see represents the truth you accept and believe. However, you may meet the person whose truth is revealed in another facet. Because you believe that your facet is all the truth you also believe the other facets to be false. In error! Of course, the other person also believes that your facet is in error.

"Then one day you have an experience that enables you to see a larger part of the diamond. The other facet becomes Truth to you now, whereas before you considered it to be error.

"We must understand that we need to observe the diamond as a whole. Let us see that all the facets are facets of truth. As we are able to open to more and more of the facets as truth the light of the diamond becomes brighter and more beautiful. Our spiritual growth takes place as we apply the principles of the truth we discover in each facet.

"The Great Master is recorded as saying 'I am the Way, the Truth, and the Life.' Some think that He presents Himself as the example only to certain religious groups. Actually He is Universal. The Christian religion has taken Him for themselves only, whereas He belongs to all. He is the example of Truth; He is the example of the Way. He is the example of the Life for all peoples, regardless of their religious persuasion.

"Truth guides you to live your life in accordance with the highest standards. It will be instrumental in shaping your life so that you may become a better and more meaningful person. It doesn't depend upon your acceptance for it to be truth. Truth is truth whether you believe it to be truth or not. Truth is truth whether you practice it in your life or not. When you do practice it faithfully in your daily life, it becomes truth to you in a very real way.

"But there is also a counterpart to this, which I will only state now and explain at another time. I hope it will give you something to think about, and here it is. Truth overemphasized can also lead to error. No, no! No questions at this time; let's reserve that to later.

"This is the end of this session. The other five subjects I intended to cover will have to wait for our next session. Those of you who are visitors may leave and attend other instructions, or visit some of the interesting pavilions available to you. The rest will return for more detailed assignments, which will be given after we take a short break."

Everybody got up and made their exits through the many doors available. It would take some time before the auditorium would empty out. While waiting for that to take place, I was thinking about what I had just heard in this class. It reminded me of a dream I had many years earlier, shortly after I had been caught in catastrophic national aerospace layoff. In the dream

I had been in a huge classroom seated in the back row high up in the balcony. It seemed that the class I had just attended was a replay of the dream so long ago. Certainly that dream was a precursor of the learning period I was entering.

As we made our way with all the others, I began sharing some thoughts with Asne and Jacob. "You know, there was a time when I was certain that I knew all of God's plan for humanity. That I had all truth. Michael O.B.Noxious reminded me so much of how I used to be. One day he is going to discover, just as I did, that in fact he knows little to nothing.

"The prospect of having to accept other aspects of the truth was frightening. However, once Doris and I opened ourselves to more truth, we began to discover there were a handful of people in our circle of friends who were thinking along the same lines. It was very helpful to have others with whom we could discuss these new concepts."

"At least you were given opportunities to move forward in your spiritual growth," Jacob added. "I believe that I went as far as I could in my environment."

"Yes," Asne agreed. "Jacob and I hope that we can move forward more significantly in our next Earth experience."

"Listen!" I reminded them. "It was easier for me than for you. I was taken away, by the uncertainties of a World War, from the influences of the religious traditions and family pressures. Both of you were surrounded by those influences. The forward move you each made in your own way was remarkable enough!

I'm sure your next Earth life will be an exceptional experience for you."

"Not only that," Asne remarked, "it's important that we keep ourselves open now!"

Both Jacob and I agreed heartily.

"Now," I asked eagerly, "where do we go from here?"

"We're to meet the scholar from the Angelic Kingdom," Asne replied. "I'm waiting for a message so I'll know where to find him. As soon as I know where the presentation is held, we'll be on our way."

Chapter 8

The Angelic Kingdom

As the class was exiting, Asne heard her name paged over the public address system requesting that she come to the front of the auditorium. She made her way through the crowd and returned a few minutes later. She was very excited and could hardly contain herself as she spoke.

"I had put in a request for you to be allowed to meet someone from the Angelic Kingdom while you were here, Aron. They promised to let me know. Just now I was told that the visiting scholar from the Angelic Kingdom is waiting for us outside. I'll recognize him because we met on an earlier occasion when I had applied for admission to the Angelic School."

I nodded my head and remarked excitedly, "Great! I'll actually meet someone from the Angelic Kingdom! I'm all ears for what he has to tell."

"As soon as we get out of this auditorium we'll look for him." Asne went on. "I was told that there would be a small group of people already with him who also are eager to hear what he has to say. Let's hurry; we sure don't want to miss anything. By the way, Aron, have you ever seen an angel on the Earth plane?"

"Yes--I have," I responded thoughtfully.

"I'd like to hear about it." Asne urged. "When and where did it take place, and how did you know it was an angel and not just someone who was still in the physical body?"

"To my recollection," I began, "I have seen an angel only once, and that took place while Doris and I were traveling in Europe with some friends. They had bought a car in Sweden, and for five weeks we drove together throughout Europe.

"At one time, when we visited Salzburg, Austria, we were going to have dinner at a restaurant called 'Peterkeller.' It was dark when we arrived, and we had to walk through a cemetery in order to reach the restaurant. It was all very strange to me.

"After dinner we got into the car and tried to find our way back to the hotel, which was outside the city. But we soon discovered we were lost. By then it was 11 P.M., if I remember correctly, and the streets were deserted, so there was no one we could ask for directions.

"Then suddenly a car drove up; the driver rolled down his window and asked, in English, if we were lost. We confirmed it, and without asking any questions, not even as to where we were going, he just said, 'Follow me.'

"He drove ahead of us, and at a fork in the road he pointed out of his car window to a road we should take. We wanted to thank him, and wave good-bye to him, but when we turned to look for him there was no one there! He and his car had disappeared as suddenly as he had materialized to extend his assistance to us.

"A few hundred feet down the highway that we were directed to take, we found our hotel. I will always remember that incident. I'm still puzzled as to how he knew we spoke English. The car had Swedish license plates, so how did he know? To top it all, how did he know that we were lost--and where he was to take us? All he said, as you remember Asne, was 'Follow me.' Is that the way angels operate?" I had often wondered about that episode, and perhaps now I might find some answers to this.

"That is interesting," Asne said. "You see, being an angel he would know what language you spoke, and also that you were lost. But he had to ask you the question so that you could admit that you were lost, thus opening the door to his help.

"The angel you encountered was a very advanced one, and as you discovered, he knew what he was doing. There is so much I can tell you about angels and how they advance in their own ranks, but there isn't time for all that now. By the way, this visiting scholar from the Angelic Kingdom will give a presentation on angels, of course. Perhaps at some other time you can visit the Angelic Schools and see for yourself how it all works. Maybe he'll invite you for a visit, but it's best not to count on it. From what I've heard, it is all very interesting and challenging. I hope you understand what I'm trying to tell you about angels?"

"I do understand," I insisted, "and I'm very eager to hear his presentation! Now tell me Asne, are visiting angels so different from departed souls who return to look in on their loved ones? They all come from the same place, like heaven, don't they?"

"Many angels are souls who have advanced to a high state of consciousness." Asne agreed. "To become an angel a soul has to go through a selection process that begins on the first level of heaven, and continues on into the third heaven. Even so, a soul who has been selected to become an angel can only advance to a certain level. The top positions in the Angelic Kingdom are reserved for those who have been created to be angels.

"However, in the great plan of this creation, room was left open for souls who desired to advance from 'garden variety' souls to the status of angels. Yet when an ordinary soul reaches the status of an angel, that doesn't mean the soul has 'arrived.'

"The responsibilities are immense and the duties are manifold. An important aspect of carrying out one's duties is absolute obedience to the assignments. From what I've heard, that can sometimes become difficult.

"You can imagine that there are many applicants to the Angelic School, but only a few are selected. You may recall these familiar words, 'Many are called but few are chosen'? Those words apply here also. For many souls are called to be angels, but only a few qualify. These souls are trained in the fourth heaven. That's where the Angelic Schools are located."

"Fourth heaven, you said?" I responded with a cautious interest. "Some Earth teaching is that there are three heavens. The third heaven was mentioned by the Apostle Paul. Are you absolutely sure of the fourth heaven?" After a short pause I slowly said: "Please--go on." I wanted to hear all she had to say, although I wasn't too sure if I really wanted to subject myself to so much new information all of a sudden. I wanted to think about every statement, as well as meditate and pray about it to make sure it gave a familiar and secure response from within.

Asne smiled at me, and with a glint in her eye she said, "As you know, there are seven heavens. Don't be surprised at my statement. There are more things in Heaven of which you know very little, or nothing, about. I'm sure you've heard the expression, 'In my father's house are many mansions.'"

I nodded. I wanted to hear the rest.

"The many mansions spoken of," Asne said, "are, among other things, the seven heavens. You can look at it as one Heaven, but with many compartments or mansions.

"By the way, the instructions on the second level and beyond are intense. The requirements and responsibilities increase in direct proportion to the light you have received. The more light received, the greater the responsibilities."

I looked at my sister as I asked inquisitively. "How can one get to the second heaven, and all the way to the Angelic School?"

Asne replied, "The way to advance to the various levels of Heaven is by being true to yourself, be of help wherever you are, and express the love of God in whatever you do. Each one has certain personal requirements to fulfill before moving on to the next level, or next heaven. So from that standpoint, anybody who has the will, who has the desire, who has the stamina, can become an angel. However Aron, you know that becoming an angel is not the only way to obtain maturity and wisdom.

"Becoming an angel is not necessarily the ultimate. There is much more to life than just that. Even those who have advanced to the state of angels can move on and prepare for other tasks just as useful. And by the way, angels don't necessarily have wings. However, if you want to think of them as having wings, that's fine. I'm sure they don't mind that. They will even appear with wings when necessary."

I kept on asking. "Does anybody ever flunk out of the Angelic Schools, or for that matter from any of the other schools on the various levels?" I wanted to know every detail of how the administration worked on the other side, so that I could be prepared when I arrived in Heaven sometime in the future.

Asne was quick to respond: "Yes. Unfortunately, candidates do flunk out, and they are sent back to their former level. In the case of the Angelic Schools, candidates who flunk out may apply again sometime later. When they do, no privileges or favoritism's are extended to them for having been there before. They are considered as brand new candidates and brand new students. They have to go through the same rigor of the entrance exams as any other candidate, and show proof of their accomplishments on the level from where they applied.

"In addition they have to produce the proper recommendations, and after that, wait for the results. There is no assurance that they will be admitted.

Sometimes they are, and at other times they are rejected. There are no limits to how many times a candidate may apply. Just remember to keep in mind that not everybody is cut out to be an angel. Nevertheless, there is no disgrace if a soul is not admitted to the Angelic Schools, nor is there any shame if a soul flunks out. A soul learns to accept the outcome with love and thanksgiving."

"How about those who are called 'fallen angels.'? Are they different from the other angels?" I asked.

"Those who are designated 'fallen angels' won't be 'fallen' forever. You see, they have fallen from the seventh heaven all the way down to the first heaven. Some even had to return to Earth. However, eventually they will all be restored to their former state if they wish, including Lucifer."

I looked startled at this revelation.

"Don't look so surprised, Aron. There is more grace and forgiveness in the Universe than you can imagine.

"Of course when the 'fallen angels' desire to be restored to their former position, that is, as authorized angels, they first have to progress to the third level of Heaven before they can apply for admission to the fourth heaven Angelic Schools. They'll have to go through the same process as other candidates, and take the chance that their applications may not be accepted. No special privileges are given to anyone, not even to them.

"Considering the number of openings available and the multitude of applicants, they may have to wait quite a while before they are accepted."

"How come you know so much about the Angelic Schools and their admission processes, Asne?"

"I applied there one time, but my request for admission was denied. I was, and still am, on the first level of heaven, and I wasn't aware of the requirements. I spotted a poster in one of the bookstores announcing the beginning of a new semester of the fourth heaven Angelic Schools. I didn't bother to read all the requirements.

"When the visiting scholar was here on one of his tours, I handed him my application. After he questioned me briefly, he explained all the requirements, and advised me to read everything on any posted announcements hereafter. That's when I discovered all that I have been telling you. In due time I may apply again, after I have reached the third level of Heaven.

"A soul may become angelic material on the first level of Heaven, but further growth in the second and third heavens are needed before an application is actually considered. Anything else?"

"Yes!" I responded. "How come an announcement for the Angelic Schools, which is on the fourth heaven, was posted on the first level? Wouldn't that be premature, especially since no one on that level could qualify?"

"The announcement was posted to make all souls on the first level of Heaven aware of these opportunities. In that way those who are interested can begin their preparation for the Angelic Schools as soon as possible."

As we talked we followed the crowd from the auditorium and came out into a very large courtyard filled with tropical plants and exotic birds. This was completely different from the place where we had entered. The fragrance from the many varieties of flowers permeated the air. This brought back memories to me of the time when Doris and I had spent a vacation in Hawaii. It had been like a spiritual experience for us that we never forgot. "This I like," I remarked. " would like to stay here for a little while, yet I don't want to miss hearing about angels."

"Why is that?" Asne questioned.

"So much has been written about them, and a number of people have told of their angelic encounters; I have wondered for a long time what type of creatures they are. How did they become angels? Have they always been angels, or did they earn their wings? How do they know what to do and where to go to help people? And how do they manifest themselves physically, and then all of a sudden disappear? Already, Asne, you've just given me a lot of information about angels. There is much that I'd like to know about them; perhaps the scholar from the Angelic Kingdom could answer some more of my questions." I responded.

"Let's keep an eye out for a small group of people," Asne urged. "We want to find the angelic scholar right away."

She looked around and spotted a group gathered in a corner of the courtyard. "There he is. Let's go! Aron, I'm sure you'll like his presentation."

"Good! I'm really eager to hear what he has to say." I responded, following closely behind Asne and Jacob.

The session was about to begin as we approached the group. With a smile the leader greeted us. Motioning to Asne and Jacob, he said "So good to see you!" Pointing to me, he continued, "This must be the brother you told me about."

Turning to the group he began his presentation.

"For now I will only give you an introduction to angels and their realm. In the short time I can spend with you, you must realize that I can only give you a quick overview of the Angelic Kingdom and how it functions.

"Originally when the Angelic Kingdom was created, there were three angels in charge of that kingdom. It was not to be considered their own kingdom, for they were still responsible to God. The names of these three angels in charge were Michael, Gabriel, and Lucifer. When Lucifer was cast out, Ariel took his place. But Ariel's position is not permanent."

"What do you mean by that?" I asked.

"Ariel will only occupy that position until Lucifer is restored to the former position for which he was created."

"Will he, at that time, recognize the error that caused him to be cast out?" I questioned.

"There is no doubt about that," the scholar replied. "When he is restored he will have repented of that great error of a long time ago. The same goes for those angels who followed Lucifer. They may all be restored. Ariel will at that time be given another mission.

"So as not to confuse you," he looked at me, "I'll take a different approach to the Angelic Kingdom. That way you'll have a better appreciation for, and understanding of, its entire operation.

"To start with, most angels are souls who have committed themselves to the rigorous training given in the Angelic School. During this period they are called angelic candidates. This training is one of many preparatory courses toward becoming an angel. As you know, this school is on the fourth level of Heaven.

"After the candidates pass this training, they are then transferred to a sub-level of the Angelic Kingdom. Here they will be novices, because they will be on probation for a period of time, and undergo further training that is more difficult and strenuous, compared to the course work they completed in the Angelic School. They are still candidates, though now on probation in hopes that one day they may be accepted into the Angelic Kingdom. They are taught by certified angels who will give them a number of difficult tasks to complete. It is then up to each candidate as to how long the training will last.

"Upon completion of this training, those who pass are initiated into the first level of the Angelic Kingdom. Here they are called angels in training.

"Angels on this level may be in training for a long time, for they still have some human tendencies that don't fit the character of angels. It is important for them to learn not to allow their love for the souls they are to serve to interfere with what they understand is best for that soul. Their motives must still be examined.

"Commitment, as you can understand, has a high priority, as does the desire to be of service.

"On this level they are taught all the ministries of the Angelic Kingdom. They become acquainted with the duties of the messenger angels, the guardian angels, the guiding angels and the search and rescue angels, and their many responsibilities.

"Having been admitted to this level, the training will include a practical experience laboratory, where each will be assigned to a certified ministering angel from the second level of the Angelic Kingdom. This ministering angel will then take charge of the trainee and carry out the assigned missions and errands, or perform what other duties and tasks that are required. The angel in training is only to observe how the ministering angel carries out the assigned duties, and assist when needed, ask questions when necessary, and eventually learn how to become a certified angel.

"Now, understand that the certified ministering angel can be either a guardian angel, a guiding angel, a messenger angel, or a search and rescue angel or any other specialist. The angel in training will have an opportunity later to decide what type of angel it desires to become.

"When a trainee becomes a guardian angel, it is assigned to a specific person, be it on planet Earth or some other planet. That will be its only purpose and priority, and nothing else, for as long as that person remains on the planet.

"The guiding angel has been taught what advice a soul may need, and when and how to give it; how to transmit it, and how to communicate that guidance to the individual. The guiding angel may work back and forth between many different souls.

"The messenger angel is one who gives a message and then leaves, like a courier. That angel has been taught that this is all it will be doing for the time being--to deliver a message. It is taught not to become involved with anything else, such as trying to give advice, or to assume the responsibility of a guardian angel. The messenger angel is taught to give its message only to the one for whom it is intended.

"A person usually has more than one ministering angel. There is no limit to the number of angels a person has; it can be anywhere from three and up.

"On special occasions the Archangels Michael, Gabriel or Ariel will function as messengers also. Remember when Gabriel appeared to Daniel and to Mary, and when Michael came to Gabriel's assistance? At one time he was serving in the capacity of a search and rescue angel. For the most part, however, these three are busy directing the entire Kingdom of Angels."

"What about those who feel that their guide is Michael the Archangel, and believe that he has come to them in their meditation to minister to them?" I questioned.

"Michael directs his personal assisting angels to carry messages to designated people. The Archangel Michael does not appear personally as such to most individuals. But that doesn't take away from the message. Neither does it take away its effectiveness or its importance. A message that comes from Michael has the same importance as if Michael himself delivered it in person.

"Now, coming back to the hierarchy of Michael, Gabriel and Ariel. These, except for Ariel, were created for this position and for that responsibility. That was needed in order that there be stability within the Angelic Kingdom. There is a certain order within the Angelic Kingdom, so that each angel knows what its responsibilities are. You need to know that the structure of the Angelic Kingdom is an important part of the entire creation.

"Let me now touch on the immense territory an angel may have. Not all angels go to planet Earth; there are many other planets in the Universe where they can be assigned. Planet Earth doesn't have the monopoly on beings who need angelic help. Their territory covers all the universes and all their planets.

"It is also important to recognize that although a soul has become either a novice or an angel in training, there are no guarantees that it will become a certified angel in the Angelic Kingdom. It can fail; it can give up and go back into the mainstream of souls in the first, second or third heaven; or it can return to the Angelic School and repeat the course. This is a decision that the soul itself makes. It may feel that the angelic training is too demanding, but it can try again for admission to the Angelic School in ages to come." The scholar looked around the group and asked if there were any questions.

"How can those on planet Earth make contact with their angels?" I was asking questions again.

"Become consciously aware of them," he responded. "Know that by faith you speak to your angels; by faith you perceive them, and by faith you hear them. Eventually your faith will become reality; that is, you will see your angels with your own eyes. Don't wait to speak to them until you know you can see them, but practice your faith right where you are, with the faith you have at your disposal."

The visitor from the Angelic Kingdom paused for a moment, looked at me and said in a hushed voice, "You should know that your wife, Doris, has come from the Angelic Kingdom just to help you. This was a decision on her part, because she knew that you would need her help in your present incarnation."

"I'm not a bit surprised at that." I responded. "She has been of tremendous help to me. And I'm aware that my primary responsibility is to take care of her. I appreciate so much what you have presented about angels. Tell me, is there much more to know about them?"

"What you have heard from me in this short time doesn't even scratch the surface of what there is to know." the scholar answered. "Perhaps on some other occasion you can visit the Angelic School. If that can be arranged, I myself will give you a guided tour of the facilities. Of course, you understand that I can't promise anything; we'll just have to see if and how it can be arranged."

Turning to the rest of the group he said, "My main purpose for coming down to this level is to find some souls who would have the potential for becoming angels. In addition to being a scholar I am also an Angel Scout. We have several openings for the next training session, so I have to work fast to get the candidates ready for the Angelic School. I must be on my way now. So nice to meet you all, and I do hope to see you again some time." With that, he was about to leave the group when I popped a last question.

"What do the angels look like, and how do they recognize each other? And how do they communicate with each other?"

"All angels are light beings. They recognize each other through the various coded vibrations that emanate from each being, and they communicate mind to mind with each other. When they communicate with you on the physical plane, it is by mind to mind if you cooperate, or audibly, or by strong impressions, and the like.

"The light beings, or angels, are very bright, so bright that an ordinary human being might be almost blinded by their intensity. That's why angels usually put on a human body to shield their light. That way their presence is more easily accepted. The shielding of their light can be compared to a black hole that swallows up all the light that comes into its vicinity and thus covers, or imprisons, the light. Imagine, if a black hole could ever be dissolved, think how bright and intense the light would be when it is set free from its prison. All that light being liberated all of a sudden would make the sky and many parts of the Universe look like a ball of fire. This would make it necessary for all people to cover their eyes, lest they be blinded. In addition--" and he interrupted himself, "I really must go; I'm already late for an appointment." and he left in a hurry.

"Too bad he had to leave so quickly; I wanted to spend more time with him." I lamented. "There is so much I want to know about angels."

"That's true, Aron," Jacob agreed, "but you have only a one day pass. There is still so much more we'd like to show you before you have to return. Let's find the soul who'll tell you about thought travel. He may take you on a fast trip to another universe. Wouldn't you like that?"

How could I pass that up? And with that we left for my next exploration.

Chapter 9

Time and Thought Travel

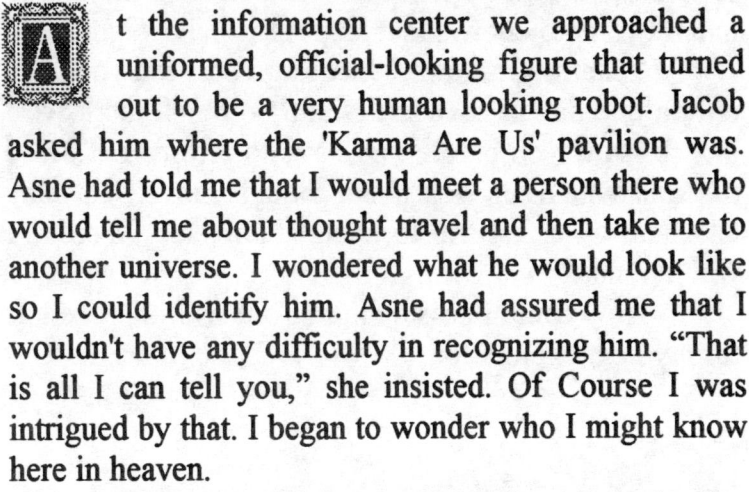

At the information center we approached a uniformed, official-looking figure that turned out to be a very human looking robot. Jacob asked him where the 'Karma Are Us' pavilion was. Asne had told me that I would meet a person there who would tell me about thought travel and then take me to another universe. I wondered what he would look like so I could identify him. Asne had assured me that I wouldn't have any difficulty in recognizing him. "That is all I can tell you," she insisted. Of Course I was intrigued by that. I began to wonder who I might know here in heaven.

A programmed answer came through as the lips of the robot moved in synch with the words. "The pavilion you are searching for is on your right, my left, about one hundred feet down Wisdom Lane."

We followed the direction given, and there it was. It was quite an impressive structure, built in the shape of a huge circle with a dome shaped roof, and constructed from white marble with huge columns supporting the large roof. The peripheral areas were open, with the wide portico following the shape of the structure. The outside area surrounding the building was landscaped in an oriental style with appropriate oriental music floating in the air, gently caressing the entire atmosphere.

As we watched the scene, we noticed that the whole structure, including the garden, slowly rotated. As it did, different types of gardens came into view. There was an Italian garden with precisely sculptured bushes and trees, and there was a Greek garden that was equally breathtaking. As the different gardens came into view, the music changed to be compatible with what was shown, Italian music followed by Greek melodies.

I had never seen anything like that, and I stood there enjoying the music and the scenery. Everything about it was very inviting, and I was interested in finding out what this was all about.

I stood there and thought on this for a while. "I think I understand it now," I exclaimed. "It's so simple, and yet so clever and complex. With the pavilion slowly turning, and the scenery changing, like a revolving stage, I can step into the Japanese, Italian or Greek culture depending upon when these, and probably many others, come around to where I am. This is like another world, or universe, existing at the same time as the one I am in. Amazing! Isn't that right?" I turned to my companions for confirmation.

"You are absolutely right, Aron. That's how it works all right, and those who are perceptive enough would be able to step into another world, or universe, at any moment. It is possible to step into the past or future, at whatever time period is desired. In that way you could examine your own past lives and also see how your future lives will turn out. Isn't that exciting?"

But this confirmation didn't come from Asne or Jacob, who were busy conversing with some other people, among them their good friend Sonja. They were so totally engrossed in their conversation there was no way that they could be disturbed.

An elderly gentleman had given the explanation about stepping into another universe, backward or forward. That man looked exactly like me. Now I knew what Asne meant when she assured me that I'd have no trouble recognizing him. We looked at each other and smiled, at the same time, and asked, also at the same time, "Where did you come from?"

"I am from planet Earth," I answered.

And my counterpart, my identical "twin," said, "I am from planet Htrae, which is a mirror image of your planet. Htrae is located outside your solar system and Milky Way, approximately 100 billion light years away. You can say we are 'far out.' But we are much further advanced than Earth in just about everything. Where I come from your people are considered to be still living in the stone age, and very often your planet is also referred to as 'hell.' My name is Nora."

"Pleasure to meet you. Your comment about planet Earth is not complimentary at all, and of no help to us on Earth" I responded.

"You are right. But it is true, isn't it?"

"Yes, I suppose so. But that doesn't mean you have to tell it like it is."

"Would you feel better if I lied and told you that planet Earth is doing just fine when it isn't? Let's go over there and sit down on that bench. My feet are tired, having been on them for over two years, as you count time."

"Tell me," I inquired, "about the universes that exist out there--or is it in there? And how do they all interact? You said you could step into the past or the future. How difficult is that?"

"One question at a time. There are presently more universes than you can imagine," Nora replied, "each with its own sun, planets and star systems. There are galaxies by the millions, black holes, pulsars, quasars, and all the rest that makes up a universe. Each universe is in gear with another universe, like wheels. It is like the workings of a large, complex clock, each part interacting with the other in perfect timing and synchronization. As one wheel turns, so do all the others in uniform harmony and cadence. It is called the cosmic clock.

"If you know about the workings of a mechanical clock, you will also understand that if one wheel stops so do the others." Nora explained. "The identical situation will take place if one universe stops moving in its orbital trajectory. But that can't happen. If it should, all the other universes would collapse on themselves and for a while disappear. It has come close to that because of the negative disturbances from a number of planets such as Earth.

"You may not know this, but there are presently space ships orbiting your solar system. Some have come close to Earth for the sole purpose of detecting negative salvos, like thought forms, and alerting the other galaxies and universes so that countermeasures may be initiated. These space ships are not just observing the actions of people on Earth, but are checking to see what the planet is up to, so the rest of the universes can protect themselves and be able to survive.

"Oh yes, while I remember," he continued, "there are a number of planets like yours in our many universes, and it appears that they are all playing an old game called, 'Can you top this?'"

"I wonder," I asked, "if each universe has a definite shape."

"Each universe has a circular shape, if you can call it that. If you wonder what's on the other side of your universe, just know that there is another universe out there. But let me go on with my explanation. Am I boring you?"

"No, no! I'm eager to hear more," I responded with excited anticipation.

"The position of each universe with respect to another varies, depending upon the vibrations by which they function. For example, a certain universe may at one time be close to that of which your solar system is a part, yet may move away at a set frequency to allow another universe to come near yours. At the same time the identical pattern takes place with the other universes, so that when one universe moves to a different position so do all the others.

"In that way those who are attuned can move from one universe, solar system, planet, civilization and culture to the next one. That is why you had to pause a moment before your brother and sister took you through the time warp. It took a little time before the universe you were going into came into focus, and you could step from your solar system and universe into the one where you are now. I hope you understand this."

"Well, not exactly," I responded, "but it sounds all right. Tell me, how did Asne and Jacob know when they were approaching the time warp? Did they understand that there was some sort of schedule they could depend on, and from that make their decision when to leave? Like a train, bus or ferry schedule?"

"That's right. There is a preset schedule by which the universes move and change positions, like billiard balls, but of course in a much more orderly and timely fashion. To the uninformed it may appear that they are moving about in a random manner, and therefore their position is unpredictable. But if you know anything about randomness, you will recognize that there is order in the random function itself."

"Yes, I understand about order in randomness, but there is much about this I don't comprehend. However, don't let that stop you. Please go on."

"Those who are able to move from one time frame to another," Nora continued, "like going from one universe to the other have this schedule programmed in their minds, although sometimes they carry a small calculator with them where all the schedules are programmed. It is similar to a tide table. Are you familiar with the cycles of the high and low tides that vary from season to season?".

I nodded, "Of course, I've lived much of my life by the waters."

"Good. Then you'll understand the rest perfectly well. Depending upon where you want to go, you just refer to your built-in time schedule and wait. At the appropriate time you step into the revolving universe, like stepping onto a carousel, and away you go.

"Another item that may interest you is that everything that has taken place, for as long as the universes have existed, has been preserved. Each soul develops an essence, similar to a spiritual DNA, during each life experience. This essence includes all of the events and situations experienced by the soul. You also need to know that at the time you call death, this essence is deposited in a universal library on a planet of the universe where all the past is preserved. I'm sure you recognize this as The Great Library which you visited earlier today with Renee as your guide. Any of the events in a person's past can be reviewed and 'lived' over again. This is what you would call traveling back in time.

"You can compare it with playing a CD on your disc player, where a number of CD's can be loaded. You can click onto a specific CD, similar to a universe in this case, and then program a particular event to play. This is similar to a planet you may want to visit. That way anyone who knows how to do time travel can in that manner visit the past and try to learn from it. The past of course can actually be changed by reconstructing it in meditation through a process that you call memory healing. Since this can also be done while still living on planet Earth, as in your case, it is always better to heal the memory before you pass through the death experience.

"The future can also be changed, for it is no more cast in concrete than the past. For prior to entering each Earth life cycle, you, with the aid of your counselors, have laid out several paths from which you can choose during that life. At that time you are reminded of the wisdom and knowledge from the past already stored in your soul memory bank. You may draw on this, if you wish, as you go through that life cycle. So many forget to make use of this. When you choose a certain path in life, you then begin to develop the actual essence that will be preserved for your past.

"You know, Aron, all of this is just a very brief explanation of what your life readings have alluded to on the subject of how a soul, just prior to entering a new life on Earth, is allowed to 'see' the parents and life experiences which it could encounter. Shortly I'll be taking you to visit a small part of another universe.

"Now, your last question on how difficult it is to step from one universe to the other can be explained like this: it's easy when you know how. The secret, which really is no secret, is to develop your inner being and be attuned to the principles of the universe. There are such things, you know; namely, a code of conduct for the universe.

"Developing this ability is no easy task, and to go a little further, it may take anywhere from many years to many lifetimes. Those who seem to 'fall' into it easily have worked on it in past lives. There is no such thing as instant success if that's what you are looking for."

"What determines how long it will take to develop this talent, or skill, or whatever you call it?" I asked.

"For your information it is called 'Normal Living'! This way you can travel with your body, and no one will know where you have come from and no one will know to where you are going when you leave, unless you tell them. As you can readily see, this would be less expensive than using airplanes, like on your planet Earth, and no reservations are needed. Whenever you are ready to use the time schedule, you go, or fly, or whatever you want to call it.

"The time it takes to develop this depends on how determined you are, how sincere you are, and what your motives are. Desire alone won't do it, but dedication and commitment will go a long way. There is nothing so extraordinary about this; it is only a matter of bringing to the surface what is already within--provided, of course, you believe it can be developed. Your faith in this can be of great help in bringing thought travel to fulfillment in your life."

"You mean that this can be developed within me as well? If that's so, where do I sign up, and who will be my teacher?"

By now I was very excited. This is what I had believed, for a long time, might be possible. I had envisioned traveling from one universe to the other at the lightning speed of thought. To see other civilizations and cultures, to witness their advances and how they are able to live together in peace and harmony, and learn from them, had been my vision for many years. And now I might actually have a chance to see this dream come true. It didn't take me long to turn to Nora and ask: "Would you be willing to take me along with you to another universe, or is it possible to do that?"

"Of course, as you wish."

"Before we leave do I need a pass to get in wherever we are going? How long will the trip take? How can I travel like you?" I was full of questions.

"This is only a demonstration so you can hold on to me; whatever you do however, don't let go. If you let go, you may end up in a different place, and I may not be able to find you. Without me you won't be able to get back here. You won't need a new pass to gain admission there. The one you have now is like a transfer used on the street cars and buses on your planet. In fact, your present pass--" he took a closer look at it-- "although it is valid for only one day, can get you into a number of universes."

"How do I know if I can trust you? You might get me lost in some universe and forget about me. You wouldn't do that, would you?"

"Of course not. You can rely on me. If you don't trust me, don't go." Without waiting for an answer Nora took out a device that looked like an electronic calculator.

"There should be another universe coming around in exactly 15 seconds, and we'll be back in less than one hour, as you count time." He looked at his cosmic tide table to verify the time of arrival of the universe. He stood up and told me to get ready. I quickly took hold of Nora's arm.

Chapter 10

Visit to Another Universe

Within a few seconds we stepped into a very different world, at least for me. We found ourselves on the outskirts of a city. We stepped onto a moving sidewalk, which being like a conveyer belt, quickly transported us into the city. We got off at city center where we asked for a guided tour.

"What would you like to hear about?" asked the guide. "There are many choices: the government in operation, the school system, financial market, or whatever else you might like. Which will it be?"

"The government, and how it functions," both of us responded simultaneously.

"But first," I hastily interjected, "I'd like to ask if you have any knowledge of planet Earth, which is where I come from."

The tour guide looked at us curiously, studied our faces for a little while, and shook his head. "Are you identical twins?"

"No, we just look like it; we aren't even related--I think" I replied. "I'm from planet Earth and he is," pointing to my companion, "from the planet Htrea, wherever that planet is. You have heard of Earth haven't you?"

"Don't remind me," the guide responded. "Earth is the only planet we know of that has caused so much trouble, in this and all the other universes. The thought forms your planet generates go, for the most part, from negative to plain miserable. But of course we have seen some very positive and enriching ones too.

"In case you don't know what a thought form is like," he continued, "go to one of the classes, where you just came from, called 'Think Right, Live Right.' I used to teach it at one time. We can't understand how good and evil can come from the same source, such as your planet Earth. These negative thought forms have ricocheted throughout the entire cosmos, and have caused a great deal of destruction to everything they have touched. It is like a disease or epidemic. When are you going to stop that stupidity and foolishness? You may not know it, but we consider Earth the insane asylum of the cosmos, and from what we see it is evident that the inmates are in charge.

"From observing these thought forms we can only conclude that there must be a lot of dissension and disagreement there. But I could be wrong."

"No you are not" I replied. "There is a lot of everything there, some good and a lot of it not so good. I wonder myself when we on planet Earth will learn to live in peace and harmony. Do you have any thoughts on that? By the way, do you have a name by which I may call you?"

There was an awkward silence. It was quite obvious that the tour guide hesitated to state his name.

I broke the silence by asking if I had embarrassed him. At first no answer came from the tour guide.

"Of course not; I am not embarrassed. It just took a little time for me to gather my thoughts so I could give you a practical and understandable answer. If you must know my name, at one time I was known as Marcus Tullius Cicero, and I lived in Rome. I hope you have read some of my writings?"

"Yes, of course I know of you, and I have read some of your works. But how can you be a tour guide when at one time in Rome you were a leader and statesman? You deserve better than this. Obviously those in charge here aren't aware of your talents."

"You must understand," Cicero answered, "my life in Rome was like a stage play. All life experiences are like that. The role I had in Rome was as a role in a play. I auditioned for the part before I came to Earth, and from the reviews I received, I think I did pretty well. Now the play is over. The curtain has gone down for the last time; the scenery has been long gone, and so have all the other actors and actresses. We are all doing something different now.

"For the present time I am tour guide, and there is a spiritual principle here. Perhaps you can figure it out. We can't always be a star on the stage, but must also be willing to do other things, to take other roles. For everything that I do, with the right attitude, is important to my own growth.

"Let's come back to your original question. You see, the planet you come from is quite young, not more than 15 to 20 million years. Planet Earth has been populated with homo-sapiens for no more than about 5 million years, or so the experts would have you believe. Before that there were huge animals that dominated the entire earth surface. The first people to visit your planet came from what you have designated as outer space, in vehicles quite foreign to your technology. They didn't like what they saw, and after a stay of 1 million years, most of them decided to leave.

"When Earth's population finally stabilized, they began to develop a high state of technology, but unfortunately they made progress their god. Because they had cast aside the necessity of obeying the principles of the universe, the code of ethics and conduct, they eventually went through some gigantic catastrophic upheavals. Several continents were destroyed, among them Atlantis and Lemuria, although it was not by destructive actions, such as underground explosions or earthquakes alone, but also by destructive thought forms generated by the people.

"Through those actions they bound themselves to a karmic wheel, and after many, many lifetimes have returned again in this century to see if they can handle similar circumstances in a more positive way. Some have definitely progressed; others are still working on it.

"Those who destroyed Atlantis and Lemuria are again back on planet Earth. If they don't make better progress, they are liable to repeat the same mistakes.

"One reason that a large part of Atlantis went into the sea was that some scientists and geologists had started to conduct some experimental explosions in seismic fault lines, which really wasn't smart thinking in the first place. They assured the population that there was nothing to be concerned about--but how wrong they were!

"The experiment got out of hand and they disturbed some very long fault lines. The result was severe earthquakes, tremendous inundations, powerful tidal waves, and a large portion of Atlantis started to sink. Those who were in charge of the experimental explosions perished as well, and these plus many others, are back on Earth, going at it again.

"It seems that it takes many, many ages of living before the homo sapiens will begin to learn. Where you come from most everyone has a long way to go. But don't give up hope; they are learning. All have to try to do their best, and if that fails, try, try again. Because those on Earth are so slow to learn, they continue to return. We on this planet wonder, in a humorous way of course, if they have all purchased commuter passes because of the many roundtrips they have made.

"We don't really make fun of them. We are just sorry for them that they are going through all of this pain and difficulty when they really don't have to. We wish we could help them by taking them out of that environment, but that really won't be helping them. They will have to learn and grow in their own way. Everybody here did, and we all spent some time on Earth. It wasn't always pleasant, but we were able to get off the wheel of karma, and continue with our progress. But we keep in mind that although we have advanced this far, there are no guarantees that we'll stay on this level to continue our growth. If any of us should refuse to live up to the light we now have, we could just as easily find ourselves back on square one starting all over again."

"I understand what you are saying," I interjected. "It would be unfortunate that anything like that should happen. How sad it would be for a soul, having progressed to a high state, to fall back to the lowest level. Many think that once you have accomplished resolving karma, you are safe. That just isn't the case, then?"

"Some souls do fall back," Cicero added, "but fortunately not too often. Since I have been here, there have been two such cases and they were dealt with very severely. It wasn't a pretty picture, and everybody here hopes that those souls will eventually learn. They were sent on a tour of duty to planet Earth.

"You see," and now he turned directly to me and looked me straight in the eyes. "The more light a soul has, the more is required of him, and of course the greater the responsibilities. There are no guarantees in the universe; no seniority, and of course no privileges. You understand that, don't you?"

"Yes, of course. It's all crystal clear," I responded. My mind raced to review my behavior, as well as my thought life. I still noticed the need to work on removing all tendencies to feel resentful towards those who had hurt me. I know I've made progress, but I realized there is yet more work to do.

I try to keep my thoughts pure, and I work on holding positive and loving thoughts. Nevertheless, I find myself being judgmental at times. I really must work on this more diligently, because I want to be sure to maintain progress in my growth.

"Here is another bit of information you should know," Cicero added. "You may have heard or read that at one time the moon that circles your planet was populated. There was an atmosphere there, not a vacuum like it is for the present. There was a shield of ionized particles surrounding the moon to protect it from the deadly radiation rays from the sun. But the people who inhabited the moon destroyed everything, and one day vehicles from outer space evacuated the entire population and found a new home for them-- planet Earth.

"The way it is going on that planet, and knowing that the sun will be extinct in about 4.6 billion years, Earth will also be emptied out. The latest reports are that a search and rescue team, consisting of many thousands of large space vehicles, adequately outfitted and staffed by a well trained crew, will be standing by for the evacuation process.

"These vehicles can travel almost as fast as thought, and they will be at the right place at the right time to evacuate all who want to leave before it's too late. How do you like that?"

"I've heard about those arrangements, and you may be sure Earth's inhabitants will be very appreciative of such a large scale evacuation effort," I said. "But may I change the subject? I'm curious about how you elect your government officials and for how long they serve."

"We don't elect our government officials," Cicero answered. "Those who are qualified--and I mean qualified--are requested to be the leaders. These are people who have shown integrity, honesty, and commitment in every facet of their private lives, and have also carried this into their public lives as servants of the people in many different capacities. You see, before a person can become a leader here, he or she must first have learned to be a servant, serving with kindness and dignity, and expressing respect for everyone.

"There is no electioneering taking place, no campaign speeches, no promises, no special interest groups, no buying of votes and no hypocrisy. Let me emphasize that we require a large measure of honesty, integrity, commitment and dedication in our leaders.

"None of those chosen receive a salary, as you would call it, from the government. Rather, the government pays the company that has employed the person for the amount of time the person is required to serve away from his or her place of employment. The company continues to pay the regular salary of this employee, and covers any extra expenses incurred while in government service. In addition, the ones who serve receive a great satisfaction in knowing that they have served with dignity and honesty. For that they earn respect from the people. As you have heard so many times, respect is obtained the old fashioned way: it is earned. For us, earning respect is much more important here than earning large amounts of money.

"The term of service for government officials is two years. We believe in term limitations here. After that they cannot serve in any government capacity for another 120 years, as you count time. When their term of office is over, they return to their former work.

"We live by a good neighbor system where communities practice watching over one another. And what you call the bartering system is also practiced here."

"You said that bartering is practiced here," I began, "but what about those who become sick and have to go to a hospital? What kind of bartering can they offer?"

"First of all there are no hospitals here," Cicero replied. "No one ever gets sick. Our healers are teachers. All our inhabitants are taught how to take care of themselves. Doctors are not needed; they are persona non grata. The healers have replaced them.

"Another thing you might like to know is that there are no jails here. Those who dare go against the principles of honesty and integrity are sent to a jail far away from here."

"So there ARE jails in this vicinity," I exclaimed. "Everything isn't perfect in 'paradise' after all? Tell me, how far away is that jail and do you call it a jail? And are there visiting hours? I'd like to go and see it. Would that be possible?" I fired the questions in a rapid volley.

"The jail is about 200 billion light years away," replied Cicero, "and it is called Earth. It is to that place we send those who have become unruly. You'd be surprised how fast they learn after they arrive there. As for visiting hours, it is open for anybody to see it and hopefully not stay too long. I hope this doesn't embarrass you!"

I nodded very slowly. I could hardly believe that this universe had marked Earth as a jail, among other unsavory names. I would have to give that some deep thought...but later.

My counterpart from the planet Htrae nudged me and said it was time to leave. We had to get back before it was too late.

"If we miss the next connection with the universe we came from, we'll have to wait an additional hour, your time," Nora explained. "I don't think your sister and brother would be pleased with that. So hurry on. You have only a few minutes for any more questions."

I turned my attention again to Cicero and said, "This is my last question. If you are able to travel to distant universes, solar systems and planets, what method of transportation do you use? What is your technology? As you know, light travels 186, 000 miles per second, which is the fastest anything can travel. Have you developed something that is faster than light? Perhaps there is something new in this kind of travel that I can bring back to Earth to further the technology there?"

"What we use here for a carrier is thought. Yes, thought travel. Your companion learned his thought travel here. He was an exceptionally brilliant student. But here we are able to take our bodies with us as we journey from one universe to another. We become one with our thoughts. Through meditation and intense concentration over a long period of training we learn to raise our vibrations to the level of thought travel.

"It isn't the easiest course to go through, but everyone here has mastered it. So if we want to visit your planet Earth, which in reality is highly unlikely, we can do so in about two seconds. Traveling through 200 billion light years in that short a time is much faster than the speed of light. Thought travel is so fast that the speed of light would appear to be at a snail's pace."

"So it is a matter of training the mind. Is that right?" I asked.

"That's right," Cicero concurred. "Becoming one with your mind. But the mind isn't situated only in your head, you know. The mind is distributed throughout every cell in the body, as well as the cells in the head. The mind in each cell is in the form of a particularly fine, high frequency energy. So in essence, when a soul becomes one with the highest vibration in its body, it needs only to make a silent wish where it wants to travel, and presto! it is there.

"To learn this thought travel takes patience and special dedication and commitment. The classes are small and the instruction intense. It's no picnic. There is a unique incentive for learning this however, you travel free, at your leisure, and in your own time."

I remarked that it would be a wonderful experience to learn to do this. In fact, it would be a dream come true for me.

"A few people on the Earth plane have accomplished this, but it is a rare occurrence," Cicero added.

"We have to leave right now," Nora broke in. "Aron, remember to hold on to me!"

Together we took a few steps, and then disappeared from Cicero's sight.

Chapter 11

Karma Are Us

A long distance had been covered but oh, how quick it was. I had hardly taken two deep breaths, and the trip from the other universe was over. "Yeah," I mumbled to myself "thought travel was something to consider. If I could learn to do that, I could teach it to others and travel like that would then be possible all over the world. No airline reservation needed; no hotel reservations, for I would come home every night no matter where I was. And the price for such travel was a real bargain -- free! Which was the right price.

"Before I leave this place" I thought, "I'll have to find out more about it. Maybe there is a bookstore around here where I can obtain some instructions on how to go about it. A 'How to Book' on 'Thought travel' with ample illustrations and practical examples. That would be almost like instant knowledge about this technique. I sure hope the book won't be too thick. I would want to learn this as quickly as possible."

I looked where we had left Asne and Jacob and they were still talking with their friends. Evidently they hadn't missed me at all. I looked around for my guide to the other universe but he was nowhere to be found. I would like to have thanked him.

"Well are you ready to go with me into the pavilion?" I looked at both Asne and Jacob.

"Did you enjoy your adventure?" Asne asked.

"It was terrific" I replied.

Being close to the "'Karma Are Us" pavilion we strolled over to it, watched as it turned in its circular pattern, and then approached the first entrance that rotated to our position. It probably wouldn't take long to go through this exhibit, or whatever it was called, so I didn't think there was any need to be in a hurry.

As soon as we entered we were met by music featuring violins. I listened to it, recognized the melody, "I Did It My Way" and then smiled. "That figures," I thought, "what other melody would be more appropriate?" As we moved farther into the pavilion the music faded. We took a good look at the place where we had entered so we could come out the same way.

We were now in an area that had the semblance of a huge lobby with marble floors, enormous marble columns reaching skyward, an abundance of hanging plants, flower gardens and waterfalls. Overstuffed chairs and sofas had been placed throughout the area in case visitors needed to rest or just sit and talk. It was very quiet here, for only whispering voices could be heard.

Asne led the way to a large reception desk where she inquired about direction to a class taught by Origen.

"That class is held in room 1285. Do you know how to get there? This is a huge place you know, and it is so easy to get lost. Would you like to have someone take you there? We have a guide available for that purpose." All this information came from the clerk behind the counter.

Asne conferred with Jacob for a moment, then turned to the clerk and asked how soon the class would start.

"You have 20 minutes before the class begins. It would save you time to have a guide take you there. Here is some information about Origen that you might find interesting" and she handed us several sheets that gave information about the teacher for the class. Asne and Jacob agreed that a guide to the class room would be a good idea.

"You may wait over there" the clerk offered pointing to a group of comfortable chairs. While waiting there I started to read about Origen to find out what kind of a person he was. I always found it worthwhile to know something about a person, especially a teacher, before I heard him teach.

The information sheets said that Origen had lived in a Christian community in Egypt. His father Leonides was martyred during the persecution of Christians in 202 A.D. It told how Origen had wanted to follow his father in martyrdom, but was prevented from doing so by his mother. She had recognized how he felt, and hid his clothes so he couldn't leave their home. At the age of 19 he took his father's place as head of the catethetical school in Alexandria, Egypt.

During his life he had been party to many debates because of his brilliant writings, which in many respects deviated from some of the teachings of the other church scholars. He had a heated debate with the scholar Candidus. Candidus argued that salvation and damnation are predestined and independent of volition. Therefore Satan (or Lucifer) was beyond repentance. Origen insisted that if Satan fell by his own will he could also repent by his own will. Origen believed that everything will be restored, and that all souls will eventually repent.

Origen was captured by the Emperor Decius in 250 A.D who was persecuting Christians. He was imprisoned and tortured. A few years after his release from prison he died from the wounds he had suffered.

While in prison Origen felt sorry for those who inflicted such punishment on him, and tried to explain to his captors that they were actually hurting themselves more than him. He knew the consequences of cause and effect (karma) and wanted to make that clear to those who kept on torturing him. But to no avail. They wouldn't listen, and besides they had orders from their superiors to carry out. Origen understood that too. Negative karma, Origen believed, is a hard taskmaster.

I thought that Origen must be quite a teacher, and I was eager to get to the class before it started. I didn't want to miss any of his teachings on karma.

"Are you the group I am to escort to Origen's class?"

I looked up, for the voice seemed directed to me.

"Forgive me for not introducing myself. I am Sir Reginald Willebough, and I am here to escort you to your class. If there is time after the class I'll be glad to guide you around this wonderful place. There is much to see and learn here."

He was a short man like 5 x 5 with a fringe of hair that was still black. He had a whisper of a mustache, a glued on smile, and wore a black morning coat and striped trousers. His shoes were almost swallowed up by a pair of light gray spats, and he sported a very fashionable walking stick. In his left hand he carried a derby hat, and dangling from his right lapel was a fine gold chain, which was attached to a pair of pince-nez. He also wore a vest with a thick gold chain fastened on the left side draping the entire front of his protruding round belly in an elegantly precise half circle, as the other end dove into a pocket where it was fastened to an ornate double-capsuled gold watch.

I was greatly impressed with the fastidious manner in which Sir Reginald conducted himself, and equated this as evidence of noble British stock. And of course he also spoke in a precise and well pointed British accent. In my eyes Sir Reginald was "top drawer."

"We take karma very seriously here," he said turning to me, "and I am sure you understand. Now let me have the pleasure of showing you around. I see you have a one day pass, and it tells me that one fourth of your time is already gone. A one day pass is a rarity here. Most visitors are only allowed to stay for no more than 15 minutes. Assuming there is time after the class with Origen, what else would you like to see? Perhaps you'd care to visit another class, or a workshop on karma? There are many sessions taking place simultaneously, and I'll guarantee that you'll find them quite extraordinary, even fascinating and informative."

"Of course. It might be interesting to sit in on a few more sessions provided there is time, and as long as I can learn something." I responded.

Sir Reginald became very enthused that he had "convinced" me to participate in one or more of the regular classes.

"But I thought that you were here to take us to Origen's class on karma? Isn't that right?" I remarked.

"Good show old chap! You have the right spirit! Come along, tally ho, and all that sort of stuff, you know. There is definitely no time to squander. Follow me!" And away the four of us went.

We walked briskly down an enormously long and very wide marble clad hallway, with Sir Reginald huffing and puffing, leading the way. This reminded him of the time when he, as a young officer in the British Colonial Army, was in India leading a platoon up a very steep hill to secure a strategic position. Those were the glorious days of triumph. He remembered it well. He had spent his entire life in the British Army, and loved the discipline, the code of honor, duty, and his country above everything else. Personal relationships were secondary, his career was of primary importance.

Those soldiers under his command feared him more than respected him. He expected everybody to have the same courage that he had. Any who weakened under the strain of battle, which often turned into well planned and orderly executed skirmishes, he encouraged to stand fast. Since he left The Great Library after entering the first level of heaven he had always wondered why he had been assigned to the 'Karma Are Us' pavilion. He had considered himself to be very nearly perfect: always on the alert, loyal and committed, attributes of which he was very proud. After all, he was well educated - at Eaton.

We made a quick turn to the left and then a right one, and stopped suddenly at a massive door that was very tall and wide. Smiling triumphantly, as if he had just invented water, he said in a whisper "We are here, follow me."

With great effort and a muffled grunt he pushed open the door, looked at the three of us as if to say "Why didn't you help me?" and beckoned us to stay close.

We stepped into a class room occupied by 25 people, all sitting in a semicircle on a floor of billowy cushions. The students looked up with questioning expressions on their faces. "Won't Origen be teaching us any more? He told such good stories and gave very interesting examples of karma. Will he be back?" one of them asked.

"He will be here any moment." Sir Reginald announced as he quickly and self assuredly made his way to the front of the room. "I have escorted your guests here. Allow me to introduce them. This is Aron who is visiting from planet Earth on a one day pass. And these are his brother and sister Jacob and Asne, who are living on this plane for the time being. I beg of you to make them feel at home. They are not completely ignorant of the subject matter. Would you please make room for them in your circle?"

Everyone moved to make the circle larger while three pillows were brought in for us to sit on.

Turning to us he continued "I have another assignment so I must leave for the time being. I'll return when the session is over and take you back to where you entered this pavilion. I hope you enjoy the class. If you have time, I'll be glad to show you more of what we have to offer here." And with that he left in a hurry.

Shortly thereafter the huge doors opened, and Origen briskly walked in. His pillow was waiting for him at the head of the class. Giving his students a cheerful greeting, he took his place on the pillow and started the session.

"Karma occupies an important part of our lives. It's like breathing. You can't live without it, and you must try to live with it. There are two sides to this coin, positive and negative. As you all know, it is the universal principle of cause and effect, what you sow, you will reap. For example when you are the cause of an event, action or circumstance, the end result or affect will be in accordance with what attitude has caused it. Karma is not just somebody's good idea, it is a principle, as well as a law of the universe. It is something no one can avoid. But it is a principle that assures what consequences (negative or positive) come as a result of behavior. So we all need to be extremely aware of that before we put anything into action. Are there any questions before I go on?"

"Yes, I, for sure, have one." a somewhat timid voice came from one in the group sitting on the floor.

"What determines what consequences I will experience when I take action on some issue? For example, if I give a large sum of money to a charitable institution doesn't that alone pave the way for a positive karma? I know when I do something wrong the outcome is negative. I assume the same, but opposite, applies when something positive takes place." He quickly sat down waiting for the answer.

Origen reflected as he gave some thought to the question. In his time on planet earth as Origen he had witnessed karma in action, and knew full well its repercussions.

"To perform a benevolent, kind act as you have mentioned," Origen began, "is only half of the issue. What is of equal importance is the attitude by which the act is performed. You could give large sums of money to an institution, but with what attitude? If you give the donation with an attitude of jealousy and resentment, or pride, or any other negative attitude as you perform the good deed, it will not bring you nearly the karmic rewards it could if your attitude were one of concern and compassion, or thankfulness and joy. You see, your attitude is the vehicle which multiplies your gift in one direction or the other.

"On some occasion a mother may have to correct her child, which may involve a little spanking. Looking at the act of spanking, it may appear to be negative. Its side effects will be many times worse if the attitude of the mother is filled with resentment and a desire to get even. However if the same mother, in spanking the child, has an attitude of love, concern, and compassion for the behavior of the child, the affect of this spanking could be very positive.

"The principle of karma has deep roots and finds its way into the very soul of every person in the Universe. Just as the attitudes determine the karmic outcome of an act, so also will the law of karma plant itself in the very act as it is carried out.

"For example, an artist may have spent many long and intense hours creating a beautiful piece of art. All along, the artist has maintained a loving attitude of thanksgiving and grace, praying that whoever purchases this piece of art will enjoy it as much as he or she enjoyed creating it.

"These positive and loving attitudes become part of the art work, being embedded in every fiber and molecule of the work, setting up healing vibrations throughout the entire work of art. This in turn works as a healing object for the one who has purchased it, and these healing energies are sent out into every part of the residence. The end result could be that a healing center may be established by the one who might purchase this one single piece of art work. So you can see how great an influence for good such positive attitudes can have on people.

"Let me clarify one thought. A healing center is not necessarily limited to the healing of the physical body. This is meant for those of you who someday will return to planet Earth desiring to start such a center.

With healing is also meant the restoration of the mental, emotional and spiritual aspects of a person. These aspects must maintain a loving relationship between one another and so must be included in the healing process. Then the whole person can experience healing and oneness, and thus live a more integrated life.

"But allow me to go on. Karma can be a master or a servant depending upon how you live your life, and in what direction your attitudes are developed. It is folly and childish to blame others for the harboring of your negative attitudes. I don't see people blaming others for their positive attitudes! What is needed and must be strived for is consistency and honesty. Consistency in striving to do the best you can, and honesty with yourself, and of course, with others.

"In the course of just one life time a person can develop many karmic patterns, some negative others positive. Let us for a moment assume that people begin to resolve their many negative karmic patterns. Let us also assume that they are very eager for a resolution, and are willing to try to tackle one karma at a time.

"However, it may be difficult to resolve just one karma at a time, because so many of them may be inter-related. Thus the individual may not know where to begin this process. It probably might be the better part of wisdom to make a list of all the life patterns that would be karmic in nature and start with the most pressing one. As they resolve that one it is quite possible that other karmic patterns may be resolved as well. But at this point it is necessary to exercise caution."

No sooner had Origen said that when several hands shot up and the first one called out: "Why is -- "

"You had a question?" Origen smiled at the one who spoke.

"Why is it so necessary to exercise caution? If I, for example, have been able to resolve some karmas and I find myself having one success after another wouldn't it be better to forge ahead and resolve all the karmas I can find and get the whole thing over with?"

"There comes a point in the resolution of karmas," Origen stated, "that in our eagerness to complete that process we may become careless, believing that nothing can go wrong, and that all will work out easily. It is so easy in the course of our life to begin to take things for granted, assuming that one success should lead to another and so on. This is such a common trait found often on planet Earth.

"The answer to your question is this. In your eagerness to resolve a lot of karmas, one after the other, you may generate two or three additional karmas in the process. Though this is not what you had intended, nevertheless that's what often happens. The end result could be that you'll end up with more karmas than when you started. That's why I said that caution is required at certain points along the path of karmic resolutions.

"I now have a question for your consideration." Origen continued. "What do you think is the quickest, but not necessarily the easiest way to resolve a karma? Give it some thought before you answer."

The students got their heads together and talked in a low voice trying to find the answer. They wanted of course to come up with the right response. But as the discussion continued they all started to wonder if there really was one correct answer to the question the-quickest but not necessarily the easiest - ". Finally one student spoke up and reported that the group had an answer.

"Well what is it? I'm eager to hear what you have come up with." Origen spoke in a kind and compassionate voice. He too was working on some of his own karmas, which he had only recently recognized. But it wasn't any easier for him than for the rest of those in the class room. He waited patiently, a trait that used to be very difficult for him. Even now he was still working on improving that disposition.

"Sir, the answer we as a group have decided on is that the quickest way to resolve a karma is to forget what wrong was done. But that isn't the easiest because we can't always completely forget, and so the event or events that we have caused or experienced will continue to be part of our memory. To live with these memories, knowing that they should be forgotten is very difficult. Because of this, frustration and anger may develop into resentment, and finally grow into something worse. Does that answer your question?"

Origen listened attentively and was thinking how he could put the more correct answer to them without discouraging them. He rehearsed in his mind a number of approaches that he might use to present the answer to them. He knew they had tried to come up with the answer. Nevertheless, it was necessary for him to help them reach the correct one. He could call for a recess and deal with the issue at a later time, but that wouldn't be fair. The class needed to know right now so that they could begin to adjust their thinking about karma and its resolution. Then when they returned to planet Earth the answer might stay with them better, and not be crowded out by other ideas.

His eyes scanned one student after another looking them straight in the eyes. This was his signal that he wanted their undivided attention. He sat straight up and leaning forward started to give his reply to this one question.

"First I know all of you have given much thought to my challenge and you have shown sincerity and desire to know the ultimate answer to the resolution of negative karmic patterns. You have come very close to the answer. Though it is very simple, yet it is, oh, so difficult for most people."

The students on the floor sat up straight knowing that an answer to an important question was about to be announced. The room was silent with charged anticipation, and the students just about held their breath. They didn't want to miss anything. They were forbidden to take notes lest they become so absorbed in their note taking that they miss the importance of what Origen had to say.

"I won't keep you in suspense. The answer is, and by all means never forget it. <u>Learn to forgive!</u> This means to forgive all those who have hurt you, betrayed you, spoken against you, caused you all sorts of difficulties and pain. It even means forgiving your enemies. If you don't try to forgive you will develop attitudes that will foster resentments and the negative feelings that go along with unforgiveness, which in turn may further aggravate a bad situation and cause you illness and even disease. The end result is that through this you have created your own environment and will be living in an inner atmosphere of unresolved conflicts.

"As Aristotle once said 'when you maintain resentment in your heart, you, are keeping alive what will eventually destroy you.' To bring this into a sharper focus, someone once said that 'keeping resentments against another person is like you taking poison and expecting that the other person will die from it.' Not a pretty picture is it? But it is so true.

"So the first thing on your agenda needs to be to forgive yourself. Then ask forgiveness of others where needed, and begin to forgive those who have hurt you, and those against whom you harbor ill feelings. Of course, also ask God to forgive you for your negative feelings. Understand that you probably won't experience anything sensationally unusual right away, but don't let that stop you. Keep up your efforts, and one day you will begin to know that your willingness to forgive will start taking hold.

"At this point an internal process of healing will begin, and you will know consciously that an inner work has started. This process of healing is accompanied with God's peace, and His power will enable you to continue this practice of forgiving. An awareness of greater love and understanding will come to you, and instead of continuing to hate and dislike certain individuals you can now begin to extend to them the love that God has extended to you.

"Without a shadow of doubt the quickest, most

effective way of resolving a karma is through the process of forgiving."

Origen sat quietly for a while, wondering how the students would accept such a simple but powerful answer. Finally he said: "I wonder if any of you have any questions?"

A long, deep, hush followed.

From observing the students it was quite obvious that they were all thinking about what he had said. The silence started to become awkward and somewhat uncomfortable when a woman in a quiet, monotone voice asked "but if I forgive those who have done so much evil toward me, doesn't that mean that I agree with their acts of infamy? And does forgiveness mean that I should forgive all who carry out acts of dishonor and brutality, like dictators or murderers or thieves?"

Origen answered in a voice of love and compassion. "Forgiving does not mean that you approve of the harmful action, or that you agree with the people who committed the act. The process of forgiving is an act of obedience to God that will bring about your personal healing. And that healing will eventually manifest itself on all levels of your being. When you are able and willing, you can extend forgiveness to all people who carry out acts of violence no matter who they are, whether or not you know them.

"To forgive is especially difficult when you or a loved one has been victimized. If for example, a son or a daughter has been killed by someone, it becomes extremely difficult and painful to forgive the one who committed the crime. Here again there is no necessity on your part to agree with the act, but you do want to start the healing process within you that forgiveness brings. Without forgiving, no matter what the case is, it is impossible to experience true personal and karmic healing.

"Your forgiveness doesn't prevent the criminal from going to prison. Forgiveness releases you from karma with that person.. Wouldn't you rather not have to meet a karmic situation with that person in another life? Unforgiveness can bind you karmicly to the person or persons involved. Judicial action for the crime will take its own course. And as you will discover, forgiving is so much better than carrying the spirit of vengeance, or resentment and ill feelings within you.

"So the answer in short is to forgive, forgive and continue to forgive.

"I hope I have answered your question. Everybody is looking for justice, and there IS justice in the Universe--it is called karma. The offending person will still have to work out his or her karma, but not with you, if you have forgiven, or repented and asked forgiveness.

"Now, let's put the shoe on the other foot. Supposing you are the criminal. You have set in motion a negative karma that could follow you for many lives, if necessary, until you reap what you have sown.

"However, let us say that you are apprehended. Your victim identifies you and testifies against you. You admit your crime, and become ashamed of what you've done. You apologize to your victim and ask forgiveness. You try to make restitution in some way.

"Your victim forgives you, you are making restitution as best you can, and you are changing your life so as to become a better person. You have resolved the karma through the vehicle of grace. However, you have broken the law of the land, and the justice system requires certain penalties to be paid. If you fulfill your sentence with a loving and understanding attitude, and hold no resentment, (it is easier when you realize that your punishment was earned) you will build good, positive karma for yourself.

"Is there anything else I can help you with before we close off this session?"

"Yes sir." another student spoke up. "What if my forgiveness is not accepted by the other party and therefore no change in his attitude? And what if after I tell him I forgive him he becomes more arrogant and hostile and may even blame me for his violent action? And now the last part of my question,: is it always necessary to forgive someone face to face? What if that person is no longer available?" The one asking the questions waited eagerly for the answer from Origen.

"Could you explain what you mean by the statement 'that person is no longer available'?" Origen looked at the inquirer.

"Yes sir. Before I left planet Earth I went through a traumatic event. I don't care to go into any details but the facts are that a close friend of mine betrayed me. I had trusted him explicitly, but evidently he broke his promise to me, and caused me much pain and heartache. After the event I never saw him again, and then I heard that he had passed over to the 'other side' as it is commonly called on planet Earth. I wanted to forgive him for his misdeed towards me, but how can that be done if I am not in contact with him? Some sort of practical explanation would be very helpful, for this event has troubled me greatly. It has left an indelible mark on my soul structure, as you can all see from the big, ugly gaps in my aura. While on earth I thought of it often, and I still do." He closed off his remarks and looked to Origen for the answer.

Origen began his response with "Your desire to forgive, with the resulting process of healing the karma being set in motion, does not depend upon the willingness of the other person to accept your forgiveness. You have extended to him your offer of forgiveness. If he refuses it that is strictly his business, not yours. He will suffer the consequences of his own rejection of your forgiveness. But you must continue to love him with the love that God has given you, regardless of his action. He will sooner or later learn from someone else some very hard lessons. If he should become more arrogant after you extend forgiveness to him, that is his business. He is responsible for his actions, you are responsible for yours. Always keep in mind that your forgiveness does not mean that you approve of his actions and behavior.

"Now to the last part of your question. You can forgive someone who has gone to another world simply by saying 'I forgive you' and then mention the person's name. Your words will travel to where that person is located, and he will know that you have forgiven him. What he does with this potential process of healing for himself is up to him. You can't force him to accept it, that must come voluntarily from him. The same principle applies no matter where the individual is, whether in the physical or non-physical plane. From this, I am sure it is made quite clear that you don't have to have a face to face encounter with someone you want to forgive. I hope this is clear."

Turning to the rest of the class he said: "Thank you for being so attentive, and now we are ready for a recess. But before we break up, let me remind you that this class will resume in 60 minutes, as you count time, when we shall have some practical experiences in forgiving. While on this intermission discuss what you have heard and see if it makes any sense to you. We shall talk more about this in our next session. Make sure to return, and by all means be punctual. Sir Reginald is waiting outside, and will escort our visitors through the pavilion so they can find their way out of this complex. Class dismissed."

Sir Reginald was waiting at the door for us and while walking down a long wide hallway I remarked "Interesting class. By the way, Sir Reginald, how do you know your way around here? You must have a photographic memory or something. How many class rooms are there in this pavilion and where do -- ?"

"You ask too many questions old chap, but nevertheless I shall answer them to the best of my abilities.

"I find my way around here by following the magnetic and computerized lines imbedded in the floor. I have a mini-micro computer in the breast pocket of my jacket, and while I was waiting for you I programmed it for the nearest exit door.

"Having done that, I follow the lines in the floor by listening for the signal that directs me to the nearest exit door. Long before I have to make a turn I am told about it through my computer. You see, the lines in the floor are like, but not identical to, what you on planet Earth call fiber optics. This allows for thousands of different directive messages to pass through these lines without any interference at all. Simple isn't it?" he smiled.

"For your second question there are exactly 8000 class rooms in this pavilion, plus 3000 demonstration laboratories and 1200 areas where everybody can congregate to discuss what they're learning. Anything else? I see from the schedule I have that there won't be any time at all to show you any more of this pavilion. I hope you, Aron, aren't too disappointed, but perhaps someday you can return, and then I may be able to show you around."

We finally came to a huge area that was familiar to us. The same music, "I Did It My Way," was playing. We knew now how to find our way out.

"It was a pleasure to meet you." Sir Reginald put out his right hand, "Next time stay longer. This is a most fascinating place, beastly enchanting."

Chapter 12

Think Right - Live Right

As we left the pavilion I spotted three familiar souls. One of them was Sonja, the one Jacob had been in love with for many years in Norway, but never had the courage to ask for her hand in marriage. As a result he never married.

Jacob quickly moved over to her side and started talking with her, leaving Asne and me trailing behind. Sonja and Jacob were both openly interested in conversing, and it was quite evident that they had much to talk about. Asne became occupied with Oskar and Lilly, who were the other two with Sonja.

Oskar who was one of our brothers had been in love with Lilly, his cousin, since childhood, and a year after they were married Lilly died in a terrible accident. It was now over fifty years later, and Oskar had recently joined her. Needless to say they were both extremely happy to be together again.

I looked at Oskar and Lilly, and greeted them warmly.

"So good to see you!" Oskar and Lilly exclaimed excitedly almost as one voice. "We knew from the daily visitor's log that you were in this area. How do you like what you've seen so far?"

"It's fascinating!" I responded. "I really feel privileged to be allowed to visit here! By the way, I'm so glad to see you two together after such a long separation. About 50 years wasn't it? Was it a long time for you, Lilly, to wait for Oskar to arrive?"

"Not at all." she quickly said while sending Oskar a glowing smile with her eyes. "I didn't have to wait for more than about five minutes, the way we count time here, and then he followed me. You see, we count time a little differently here than you do on planet Earth. You probably won't understand it. I don't either but I accept it like it is."

"So time here must go much faster than what I'm used to. Is that right?" I responded.

"That's right." Oskar added. "That's why we can learn so much in such a short time." he said with a triumphant glint in his eye. "However this type of learning is not extended to visitors. To be on this program you'll have to reserve a seat in the classroom well in advance, and attend classes on a regular schedule.

"Which reminds me, we're almost late for a class now, Lilly. It's a very important session," he hesitated for a moment, then with a smile continued. "It's on how to improve your memory. We'll have to go. I really wish we could have more time together, but you also have much to see before you leave. Perhaps you can come visit us again.

"But before I leave I want to thank you again for giving your one share of the business to me so that

I would have a means of making living. Otherwise our other brothers would have thrown me out on the street. Thank you again, and when you come for another visit, I hope it's soon, we can talk some more." He motioned to Lilly, and away they went to their session.

I remembered when in 1938 my family in Norway decided to open another store, which was called "Textil", across the river from our main store. It was decided to issue three shares for this new store. Oskar received one, I received one, and another brother had one. To start with, I managed this business until I left for America in January of 1940.

After World War II, Oskar started up "Textil", got married again, and seemingly everything looked good for him. But our other brothers were plotting to take the store away from him, which meant he would be without any means to make a living.

When in 1958 Doris and I visited my hometown, I heard all the details about the conspiracy to evict Oskar. In order to protect his livelihood he needed two votes so that he would be in the majority. It didn't take me long to decide to give him my share, so that he could prevent any of our brothers from evicting him. I quickly signed the necessary papers, and the whole matter was settled in less than an hour. Oskar stayed in his store!

"Well, I too really have to leave you now." explained Sonja. "I must attend my music class. I have decided that when I return to planet Earth I will be a music therapist, or something like that"

"That's wonderful" Jacob responded. "Maybe in that life we'll meet again, Sonja?"

"I hope so. And when we do, don't hesitate for one moment to ask me to marry you. If you only knew how my heart ached when you kept silent about proposing to me in our last life. I waited and waited and you didn't make a move. As you know, I finally married someone else in Sweden, but I really wasn't very happy. I never stopped loving you." Sonja looked at Jacob like a forlorn puppy.

"In case you didn't know, my heart ached too. I wanted so much to ask you to marry me, but I didn't have the courage. If I had only known for sure how you felt about me, things would have been different. If I had only known." Jacob lamented.

"We mustn't allow our lives to be controlled by 'ifs.'" Sonja said. "What's past is prologue to what is to come. Let's promise each other that the best is yet to come. Is that all right with you?"

"Of course." he answered. "When we have another Earth life together again it'll be different, much different."

"You'll meet me right after class won't you Jacob?"

"I'll be waiting for you."

It was obvious they were both enjoying their renewed relationship.

Jacob watched Sonja leave and called after her "I'll be there!" The thought of her returning to Earth to become a music therapist certainly fit in with her many musical talents. He remembered how, back in Norway, she would entertain on an almost professional level with her singing while she accompanied herself on the piano.

Music therapy is a good choice, he thought. I'll try to arrange it so that I can return with her, and be her co-worker. To him that appeared like a very challenging profession. He wished it could happen right now, but he knew there were many things for him to work on before he himself should return to Earth.

The three of us stood by ourselves wondering what to do next. Not that there weren't any classes to attend, that wasn't the question in our mind, but which session would be the most profitable for me? I was reminded by Asne that my one day pass would expire shortly, so there wasn't any time at all to lose.

"Let's go over to the kiosk nearby, and check on what classes are offered and how long they will take." Asne suggested, motioning us to follow.

A long list of classes, forums, workshops and debates was posted on a large computerized bulletin board. Making a selection from such a long directory of classes would not be a simple one. I wanted to attend all of them, but knew there wasn't time for that.

"How many sessions do I have time for?" I inquired. I was hoping I would be able to attend at least two or three more classes, perhaps even more.

"You have time for one short session, possibly two. That's all. Maybe at another time, when you visit us again, you may be able to sit in on more of the instructions offered here. But for now, that's all you'll have time for." Asne looked at me, hoping that I would understand.

"But can't I get an extension on my one day pass? Surely the officials will understand, when I explain to them how much I would like to attend a number of classes. Don't you think they would?"

"They'll understand all right, but that won't make any difference with them. Remember, you shouldn't be here in the first place. Don't spoil your chances for another visit."

While answering me, Asne was looking over the long list of classes available, and then she burst out with "Ah ha, here is a class you'd enjoy. It's called 'Think Right - Live Right', and the teacher is someone by the name of Lao Tsu. I've never heard of him. Maybe he is a visiting professor from another universe, or something like that. Now, this is interesting. It says here that the class will be held in Cosmic Grove. I have seen that place, and it is unique. Let's go!" With that she rushed off. Jacob and I followed on her heels. "We must hurry to be there in time. I don't want you to miss anything. Hurry, hurry!"

Cosmic Grove was an outdoor amphitheater situated in a pleasant environment. It was a mixture of Chinese and Greek architecture. Tall, Ionic type, slender columns supported a curved roof, over the large platform where the podium stood. In the distant background the sound of cascading water could be heard adding a harmonious touch to the setting.

As we entered the area, a biographical sketch of the teacher was handed out. To me this man was already familiar.

The information read: "This sketch is based on one of the many lives of a former teacher on planet Earth, named Lao Tsu. He was a celebrated Chinese philosopher, and a contemporary of Confucius. He is known to be the founder of Taoism, one of the most ancient and important religions of China. He was born at Keuh-jin, in the district of Koo. He held office at the imperial court of Chow, in the province of Honan in the sixth century B.C. as librarian of the archives."

We took the only vacant seats left in the center section, but these were towards the back, which didn't please me at all. I preferred a seat near the front, especially in the first row center.

"You don't learn any more in the front seat than you do in the back one." Jacob reminded me. "It isn't where your seat is, that's so important, but where your brain is, and how you use it. You can listen here as well as any place. Just watch, and see what's coming."

Suddenly the entire amphitheater became quiet.

It was as if somebody, by magic, had called to their attention that the teacher was here, and it was now time to be alert to the instructions that were to follow.

Actually, somebody had communicated by thought to all the students, and that's how they knew that it was time to stop talking and start to listen and hear. But I hadn't heard a thing, I had been too busy talking, and neither had I been trained in thought communications. So in reality, there was no magic to the silence coming about. It only appeared to be, as I perceived it.

Unexpectedly a miniature Chinese man appeared right before me. This was an identical figure of Lao Tsu. "Now what?" I thought. But the Chinese gentleman smiled at me and put his index finger over his lips. A clear indication to keep quiet. The Chinese figure was just floating in the air, and he indicated that he was ready to start his lecture.

"How do they do that?" I thought.

"Keep your thoughts quiet or you'll be interfering with the lecture." This came from Lao Tsu the Chinese teacher.

"Now, let's get started. For those who are here for the first time, I welcome you. To those who have repeated this class a number of times, welcome to you also. There may be a few visitors here, and because they have a limited time to spend, I shall make my remarks brief and to the point. If any of you have questions, please wait until the lecture is over. It could be that you may find the answers you seek as we progress in the lecture.

"As you know this class is called 'Think Right - Live Right,' and this is easier said than done. You probably know by now that our thoughts shape us so that our lives, in every area, will conform to what our thought patterns are. Our thoughts are more powerful than we can ever imagine.

"With our thoughts we can will to do what is good, as well as what is evil. As a matter of fact, it takes the same energy to do either of these. Therefore it is not the thought alone that is so important, but also the direction we give it. A good noble thought in the hands of an undirected, unprincipled, and undisciplined mind can do untold damage, or produce nothing at all. At the same time, an immoral thought entertained in the mind of a directed, principled person can bring about great damage to the nobility of good character. You know that it is not the thought only with which we are dealing, but the resulting action that may come from the mind that holds the thought.

"We have within us the seed of imagination, which is the storehouse for all the creativity we can conceive. Imagination is carried on the wings of our thoughts. Depending upon our will power, the thought, loaded with creativity that is generated by the imagination, is now given direction whether for good or for evil.

"Our thoughts do not exist in an isolated state. Let us remember that, wherever we journey and to whatever Universe we may return. With our thoughts we generate a series of thought forms peculiar only to us individually. These go ahead of us wherever our voyage takes us.

"This is our signature for good or evil deeds. In that way we are known throughout the multitude of universes, and there is no way we can escape or hide from their consequences, whatever that may be. Some try to blame others for the negative consequences. But the Universe has already experienced the thought forms, and knows from whom they originated. We alone have the responsibility for our own thoughts and actions no matter what the end result.

"Though each thought creates a different thought form, it has a particular signature unique only to its creator. In just one lifetime we may develop many hundreds of thought forms. Some gentle and kind, others very ugly and grotesque. Let me illustrate to you what good thoughts will create."

He snapped his fingers, and immediately a figure of an angel playing soft harp music appeared. With tenderness the melodic notes caressed each soul like a loving mother would care for her first born.

He allowed the angel to remain for a short while so that all could appreciate and enjoy the quieting soothing music. A tranquil hush fell over the entire amphitheater, and all were at peace with themselves and everything surrounding them. He snapped his fingers again, and the angel disappeared.

"There are many other tranquil thought forms of course, but I am sure you understand that there isn't time to present all the variations of all healing thought forms. Now, I want to bring you an example of a thought form created by a cruel and destructive thought."

Again he snapped his fingers, and a hideous figure appeared. The audience gasped in fear and anguish. The peace and warmth that had previously hovered over the audience was suddenly replaced with a cold chill of mistrust and fright.

Lao Tsu quickly snapped his fingers and the thought form disappeared. But to restore the peace and unity that had been there before, he brought the angel with the harp back for a moment.

"If you thought that this negative example was repulsive, you may be sure that this is one of the better forms produced from unhealthy and evil thoughts. An interesting aspect of this is that when a person immediately changes his or her thought from bad to good or the other way around, the thought forms will also change in accordance with the last thought that is maintained. In that way one can change the outcome of one's own potential actions.

"Don't think for a moment that a thought form has a limited life and influence. Such a thought form will last for ages, and it will travel to the far distant universes influencing everything for good or evil in its path. Its influence is of course also felt on the planet where you live.

"The energy of a thought form does not diminish though it may travel to distant parts of the universes. Actually, it can gather strength when it combines with other thought forms of the same or identical values, that is, positive or negative, no matter where in the Universe it originates. From this it becomes rather obvious that the more energy a thought form is given, the stronger it becomes. Thus the more damage or good it will do, depending upon the nature of the thought form, of course. The most effective thought form for creating peace and harmony is the forgiving thought. The worst thought form we can create is that of revenge or violence.

"As you know, words and their thoughts are intertwined. We can seldom think unless we also use words, though they may be silent, but words they are.

Try it when you have a moment to spare, and you'll discover this to be true.

"Keep in mind that we are responsible for every word we think and speak. What we think we are more likely to eventually speak. This may result in our making a decision and/or taking certain actions. So the end result, I am sure you understand, depends on our thinking patterns, and how they influence our behavior.

"In that way we will be creating the environment in which we live, which may or may not resemble reality. The fact of the matter is that we don't always see things as they are in reality, but rather, as we think so we see. This is a projection of our unwillingness to perceive the truth about the world in which we are living.

"I am aware that someone has a question. Let me see how it can be properly stated. Oh yes, you are asking where the thought originates? Is that correctly stated?" A "Yes" nod from a member in the audience indicated it was correctly expressed.

"Well now, let me put it this way. The spirit, the all knowing, thought by some in various universes and cultures to be the super-conscious mind, imparts to the soul what it desires to be impressed upon the conscious mind. This is in the form of suggestions and advice only, but always the truth, not hard, fast commands.

"The soul has the responsibility of choosing what lessons and thoughts it will bring to the conscious mind, such as how it might respond to the many experiences it meets. It has the responsibility to become aware of the order of the priorities to which the conscious mind needs to address itself. Through this method several options are presented to the conscious mind. From this it can choose the one that is to its best liking at that moment.

"For every subject the conscious mind shows an interest in, there is always a ready input from the spirit to the soul. Hopefully the soul will understand the instructions from the spirit, and will direct these to the conscious mind.

"This doesn't mean that the individual becomes a robot, or that all decisions are made for you. The individual is still a free agent. He can take the advice offered, or completely ignore it and go his own way.

"No matter how the individual responds to the counsel, the end result is transmitted to the soul, who compares it with the suggestions offered. The soul, in turn, relays its findings to the spirit who compares the end result with the truth given. How persuasive was the soul in making the suggestions to the conscious mind? How well did the individual respond, so that the purpose of God could be carried out?

"The soul, acting as a go-between for the spirit and the conscious mind, may not always be in accord with the spirit. Supposing the soul becomes rebellious?

"Yet over a period of many lifetimes the soul will eventually hear the message from the spirit, and finally impress it upon the conscious mind with such persistence that the responses of the physical body will fall in line with the desires of the spirit. At that point, there will be unity in the body, soul, and spirit.

"Through these trials, experiments and attempts, the individual will eventually learn. It is the constant and careful correction, encouragement and hope, all wrapped in love from the spirit, whose message is forwarded by the soul to the conscious mind.

"The bottom line of this is that you can finally be free from prejudice, bigotry, revenge, hatred, resentment and jealousy, while still having full knowledge of being responsible for all of your actions.

"It should be pretty obvious from this that the spirit supplies the substance for the thought patterns. But the soul and the conscious mind can choose to work with the thoughts, or to discard them, or to change them. Therefore the origin of all thoughts comes from the spirit. As we can see, this is the process by which the final thought is generated.

"But even so the individual can turn a positive thought into a negative or evil one, or a negative thought into a positive one, thus making it unrecognizable from the original substance. I hope this has answered your question. Are there any other questions? We have only a short time left before this part of the class is over."

At that moment a messenger made his way quickly to the podium and handed Lao Tsu a written message. Lao Tsu looked it over and then announced: "I have just been handed an important message which is to be read aloud to you."

A stir of excitement and questioning went through the whole amphitheater. Everybody in the assembly sat straight, up and moved forward to the edge of their seats, hoping that this would make them hear better.

Lao Tsu raised his voice to make sure that everybody heard this announcement.

"Please pay attention, for this is very important. Another list of those who will be returning to planet Earth has just been posted at the Outgoing Unit Information Center. It is requested that all souls check the list to determine if their names are on it. You are instructed to follow this messenger to the Information Center. His name is Septus Terralegoff. (He, by the way, used to be a professional wrestler in his last incarnation on planet Earth.) If your name is on the list proceed immediately to the final instruction class at the complex before departure. This will be conducted by Lucien Hippopotumus, with Winston Churchill as the keynote speaker, and held in the staging area of the Outgoing Unit Complex. This is the end of the message. Those whose names are not on the list please return here as quickly as possible so that we may begin another session of 'Think Right - Live Right'. This session is now over, and you are dismissed."

The miniature Chinese figure in front of me suddenly vanished.

The amphitheater emptied quickly as the people got up rapidly and followed Terralegoff toward the Outgoing Unit Information Center. Only a few remained, including Asne, Jacob and me.

"Do you think your name is on the list?" I looked at both of them. "I sure hope you can stay at least until I have left. Otherwise I wouldn't know how to find my way around."

"Don't worry we know we aren't on the list. It'll be some time before we return." Jacob replied.

"What about those who are still in their seats?" I inquired. "Why aren't they checking out the list? Do they also know that it isn't time for them to leave?"

"I doubt it." Jacob answered. "I suspect that they just don't want to find out if their names are on the list. They have known for quite a while that their departure time was coming, but were hoping that it would never occur. They have been here for quite a while, before the American Revolution, and they don't want to leave. They told me on a number of occasions that they had found a home here and want to stay.

"The decision has been made from the highest authority to send them back where they came from. They have been here so long, and should have learned at least the basics. But no! All they have done is to play around as if this were a country club. Their class attendance has been very poor, and when they showed up for a class they paid no attention to the instructions. Their workshop participation was virtually non-existent. Need I say more?

"They had been encouraged and warned by their guides (and just about everybody here) but to no avail. Here they were given every opportunity to learn, and to prepare themselves for their next lives, but they never took advantage of it. Returning to planet Earth without preparation is doing it the hard way. And this is their choice."

"How do you know that so many had tried to help them? Perhaps they are misunderstood and need one more chance." I suggested.

"I was one of their teachers,." Jacob replied. "Only once. But there have been many other teachers before me who have tried to help them. I was their last chance. After my experience with them I requested they be demoted, for I could tell that they weren't even trying. This group has gone through more teachers than you can imagine.

"Let me assure you they are not misunderstood. We understand them perfectly. They refuse to learn, and they have had more chances than most. If they remain here they'll never learn. Back to Earth they must go, and I just hope that their experience on Earth will give them greater incentive to grow."

"Jacob, I have one more question." I said hastily. "When Lao Tsu started his lecture, a miniature Chinese figure appeared in front of me and remained there during the entire session. But as soon as the lecture was finished the figure disappeared. Is this normal?"

"Yes, the Chinese figure was a hologram of Lao Tsu, which appeared to everyone at the lecture. Because the lecture arena is so huge, and the speaker is so far removed from the listeners, the display of the hologram was used so that all could clearly see and hear the speaker. It was projected from the back of the chair in front of you. When he was finished the hologram disappeared."

"We have time for one more class," Asne reminded me, "and this one will be very short. Your time here is almost up."

Leaving the amphitheater, we noticed several uniformed personnel moving quickly toward the remaining group. They tried to scatter, but were quickly rounded up and led away to the Outgoing Unit Complex.

"We don't want to return to Earth! We like it here! We all like it here!" was heard as they were led away.

We watched as this took place. "They will be placed in an isolated section at the Outgoing Unit Complex. There they can hear the final instructions." Jacob explained.

"Is there a bookstore of some sort around here? I'd like to see what they have there." (What I really wanted was to obtain a book on thought travel.) Asne and Jacob knew it.

"Let us show you where the bookstore is." Both of them answered at the same time.

"We have the finest bookstore in all of the universes combined. You wouldn't believe what we have here!" Jacob offered. Though both Jacob and Asne knew what I was looking for, they didn't say anything.

"It is really close by. Just a short walk away." Jacob continued.

"But don't waste your time browsing." Asne warned. "If your pass runs out while you are shopping around, the security guards will come and get you. That will be the end of your visit. This means you won't have any time to attend the last session we have planned for you, and from there to witness a unique sight. Something that you may not see for a long, long time. To make sure that you get to the last class we'll go with you." Asne explained.

We approached a huge building made from marble and gold with large archways, but no doors. Evidently this place is open 24 hours a day, seven days a week, as I counted time, to service the large crowds that patronized the bookstore.

"The section of the building that contains the bookstores is in the basement. It is like a huge enclosed shopping mall." Asne added.

"Which part of the bookstore would you like to visit?" Asne asked. "There are four floors of bookstores in the basement. We have books on every conceivable subject, in all languages known and extinct, from every Universe in the Greater Universe.

"There are 40,000 bookstores in this basement. 10,000 on each floor. So tell me which section would you like to see?"

"I'd like to find a book on thought travel, if there is such a book available? That interests me greatly" I replied.

"There are many books on that subject available." Jacob replied. "Starting with a primer on thought travel, to the most advanced, which is on group thought travel.

We took the first entrance on the right, and walked toward a flight of stairs. Over the top of the stairway a big sign announced: "Welcome to the Book Cellar."

"Is thought travel a popular subject?" I turned to Jacob. "Is everybody interested in that topic?"

"Just about. But not everyone is able to obtain the information."

"Why is that? Don't they take credit cards here?"

"That has nothing to do with it. Just wait and you'll find out." Asne replied.

They led me to the fourth level, which was especially busy with a large crowd inside the first book store. A number of signs in the windows announced that books on thought travel were now available. Those interested in obtaining a copy would need to show their identification card to the clerk.

I edged my way to the counter and got the attention of one of the clerks.

"I'd like to have a copy on basic and advanced thought travel. I don't have much time so please hurry."

"You want one copy each of all the available books on thought travel?" the clerk repeated.

"That's right. Anything wrong with that?"

"Yes, there is. You can have only one book at a time on that subject. So you want the beginning volume then?"

"Yes. In that case give a me copy of the primer on thought travel."

"Let me have your identification number so I can check it with the computer data list."

I was puzzled, and questioned the clerk. "Why do you need to check your computer? Don't you have the book available? I'll be glad to give you my credit card. Which ones do you accept?"

"We don't accept any credit cards here. I have to check the computer to see if your number is on the list. Your number is added to the register only when you have completed a prescribed set of courses making you eligible to proceed to thought travel. How long have you been here?"

"I am only a visitor here, and will soon return to planet Earth."

"I'm sorry, but you aren't eligible to obtain any of these books," the clerk said apologically. "Unless you have passed the prerequisite courses, which are very rigorous, and your number comes up on the computer data base, you can't obtain any of the books on thought travel." The clerk looked at me somewhat dismayed and amused and said, "You are very ambitious, but you don't meet the qualifications." With that the clerk turned to other customers.

As we left the Book Cellar we passed a video store, and saw a travelogue from a far away Universe. But this video tape was projected through a machine that produced it in a holographic form. As we watched, it was as if we were in the middle of the scene, in full color, sound, smells, odors and aromas, which made it very realistic.

"It's time for your last session." Jacob reminded me. "You'll observe the procedure that the souls go through who are leaving for planet Earth to begin another incarnation. If we hurry we'll get in on the very beginning."

Chapter 13

Life Recycling

The lecture was already in progress when we arrived at the Outgoing Unit Complex. We entered an observation deck that overlooked an enormously large courtyard where thousands of people were standing, listening to the speaker. A Greek philosopher by the name of Lucien Hippopotumus, standing on a high platform placed in the center of the courtyard, was delivering the orientation program to those who were about to depart. Each person was holding a piece of paper that had been distributed to everyone who entered the complex. While the speaker was giving the instructions he asked each of them to study the paper very carefully for this information was vital for their next return to planet Earth.

"You will notice," he started, "that attached to your assignment sheet is a commuter pass that you will surrender at the point of departure. The number on your pass indicates how many return trips you already have made to planet Earth. This will tell you how many lifetimes you have spent on that planet. I suggest you take a close look at your commuter pass and see what number it has. Do this now so that you may know how many roundtrips you have made.

"While you are doing this, also look over your new assignment that is described in detail on the information sheet you received when you arrived here. There you will find details about the country you will return to, its culture, and the family you will join. Keep in mind that this assignment is final. There will be neither substitutions nor any changes. No one will be allowed to exchange assignments with another person. Don't even ask for it. Again, understand that your mission is final for your upcoming life cycle!"

"In the upper right corner of your assignment sheet there is either a letter 'A,' or a letter 'V'. The 'A' stands for 'assigned'. That means that after careful examination of your past lives and the progress you have made here, your teachers, in consultations with each other and with the higher authorities, in your presence and with your consent, have agreed to send you to the duty station indicated on your assignment sheet. This will be the most opportune area for you to learn to take responsibility for your actions, and for you to learn to be of service to the people around you, as well as those in your community. In this case you had nothing to do with the choice of your assignment, or where you will appear in this upcoming life. This was decided to be the best for you, and you agreed with the selection. As you already know there is no complaint department established here, and there is no budget for one either.

"The 'V' stands for 'volunteered'. This means that those who have that letter on their assignment sheet have volunteered to appear in a particular place and situation in this coming lifetime. This is your choice. Most of you have chosen the parents you prefer as the vehicle for your life experience."

He paused for a moment indicating that this part of the indoctrination was over, and then cleared his throat to get their attention. There was obviously more to come.

"Before my final remarks, I want to turn the meeting over to a very special guest speaker. We are privileged to have a person of this stature with us at this time. I have the great pleasure of introducing to you, Sir Winston Churchill!"

With that he left the podium, and a short, stocky, pudgy-faced man appeared on the stage. He looked at those assembled with his penetrating, steel gray eyes, squinting as he surveyed (almost like a radar antenna) the entire crowd . He was very serious. The audience knew, just by the look on his face, that they had better pay attention. Everybody kept silent, even those who didn't like their assignments.

Sir Winston kept turning around so that everybody could see him. One more look at them and he was ready to deliver his message to the assembled crowd.

"I have a few words for you to take with you for this new lifetime. I shan't be long so as not to delay your departure. In a few short moments you will all leave here and journey to your duty station. Your assignment will place you in a wonderful opportunity to serve, to grow, and to mature. See to it that you don't miss the challenges to overcome obstacles from which you can grow and eventually mature.

"When you come across difficulties, obstacles, and opposition, pay attention to them--for they are your teachers in disguise. When you are maligned, betrayed, or made the laughing stock, don't become discouraged. I know what I am talking about. In my last lifetime on planet Earth I experienced all of these, but I overcame them. Instead of allowing these situations to discourage you, use them as stepping stones to rise above the circumstances. Whenever you feel discouraged never, never, never give up.

"While you are on planet Earth many of us here will be watching you and cheering you on, provided that what you are engaged in is honorable and sincere. Keep in your heart that you are never alone. When you become discouraged and faint of heart, we will send you comfort and peace, and give you hope to carry on. Draw on this. When you accomplish something, no matter what it is, we will applaud you on to bigger and greater goals. You won't be aware of our support unless you concentrate, and knowingly remind yourself that we are there for you. Keep renewing your awareness of this from the very start of your new Earth experience.

"Ever so often an angel will appear to you. Don't become surprised or frightened. The angel may even come in the form of a man, or a woman, or a child, and you may not recognize it for who it is. The angel doesn't always have wings! Whatever shape the angel takes, know that it is there to encourage you and to give you hope.

"I want to give you three top priorities to hold throughout this new life cycle. The topmost priority is your dedication and commitment to God, the Supreme being. The second top priority is your dedication and commitment to your family-your loved ones. The third is dedication and commitment to your work, your career, your profession.

"These top three priorities must be kept in the order given. Other priorities fall below these. Following these priorities, and the divine principles you apply will give you clear guidance for making decisions and choices in your life, and will lead to a more balanced and more meaningful Earth experience. All this will make your next life exciting and rewarding.

"When you attend to your profession be diligent and committed to it. Don't expect the position you hold to make you a gracious and worthy person. What will make you a person of substance are the meaningful and noble attitudes you develop and apply in your daily life. The work you do will be a means to provide a living for you and your family, and will be a vehicle for expressing your attitudes. All of us here encourage you to use these beneficent attitudes throughout every experience you come across.

"Whatever you accomplish, and whatever your conquests may be, the most important victory you can ever hope to achieve is to conquer yourself. Nothing is more important than that! Above everything else don't allow your disappointments to crowd out the purpose you are to fulfill.

"Whenever you can, try to be of service to all you meet. Keep in your heart that you are your brother's or sister's keeper; never their judge. Be as happy as you can one day at a time. Remember that wealth will not bring you happiness. It can only bring you a more comfortable life. You must discover happiness in whatever situation you find yourself. For happiness comes from within, in knowing who you are.

"And let me remind you again, never, never, never give up! Thank you, and good luck in your new adventure." He waved to those assembled as he stepped down from the podium.

Lucien Hippopotumus appeared again and gave the final instructions. "You will now proceed to the departure gates that are clearly marked. I ask that you stay in a single file. There is no need to push, you'll arrive at your destination at the right time. When you move on through the departure gate deposit your commuter pass and the assignment sheet in a box clearly marked for that purpose. Commit to memory all the information on your assignment sheet.

"Prior to your exit an array of colored lights will be projected from here to Earth. Each of you will make your journey there on one or two of these rays. On rare occasions a soul may enter in on three rays of color. The appearance of the rays will indicate that it is time for you to leave. Your guides will indicate which ray of color is yours. This color also coincides with your purpose, and this will be the color or colors you will feel the most comfortable and secure with, provided you accept who you are.

Life Recycling 217

"Connected with the beam of color there will also be projected a coat of arms, which is unique to you. This is also known as your life seal. Try to remember all the symbols in your life seal, for here again you will recognize in symbolic terms your purpose, your strengths and your weaknesses, and what you need to work on. The color rays, and your life seal are two important tools given to you to help you know more about yourself and your purpose. Good luck, and pray that this time around you will accomplish your purpose. We'll see you upon your return."

The orientation lecture was over. The souls filed out of the courtyard and lined up single file outside the numerous exit doors. As they did, they deposited their assignments sheets and the commuter passes in the containers provided, and waited their turn to enter through a short passageway that would lead to their final place of departure. While walking slowly through this last hallway we could hear a melody playing over the loudspeaker system; it was "I'll be seeing you." A very fitting tune for the departing souls.

"Let's go and watch them leave; it might be interesting for you, Aron." Asne suggested. "We have watched this kind of departure a number times."

"Sure, I'd like to!" I replied. "From where can we watch these proceedings?"

"ollow me." Jacob instructed. "The departure of all these souls doesn't take very long, so let's hurry."

We went to the other side of the building and took an elevator to the observation deck where we could watch the entire event.

I blinked my eyes. What I saw was so extraordinarily colorful and unique. All I could do was to look at it without saying a word for a long time. Then only a few words came over my lips "So that's how it's done!"

"This event goes on continuously" Asne remarked.

As far as the eye could see, long streamers of colored lights, in the spectrum of the rainbow, formed a trail to planet Earth. The whole region was a brilliant display of lights. More than just a spectacular scene, it was the pathway for thousands of souls entering planet Earth on specific color rays. I watched intently, and then I saw many small, gleaming, star-like lights moving very rapidly along the pathways of the colored lights.

"What are all these stars doing on the colored paths?" I asked Asne.

"They are the souls you saw in the courtyard who are now making their return to planet Earth. Pray for them that they may be able to fulfill their purpose this time." was her reply. We stood there, and in silence watched the souls depart.

Chapter 14

Journey's End

Watching the souls entering planet Earth reminded me that it was time for me to leave. This had been a wonderful experience. Never before had I seen so much in just one day. The people I had met, the teachings I had listened to, the discussions I had been part of--all of it was more than I could ever have imagined. I needed time to digest it, think it over, meditate on it, and try to practice in my personal life what I learned from it. There were so many things I wanted to know. Even things like where the spirits of our loving faithful pets go when they leave their physical bodies.

"Asne! I haven't seen any dogs or cats or horses. Nothing of what we consider our earthly pets. How can heaven be heaven without our pet family members being there also?"

"Of course!" Asne saw my concern. "Animals have their own section of heaven. They have training sessions just as we do, to help them develop their spiritual consciousness even further. They learn to become even better companions for us. Their little hearts and minds are so much more open than ours and their consciousness is raised very quickly. When they and you are in heaven at the same time you may be together as often as you wish."

Time had passed so fast!

I still needed to talk to Asne about a matter which had been on my heart for some time.

"Before I leave heaven," I began, "I want to tell you about a dream I had a few years ago. What led up to this experience was my concern about crossing to the other side at death, only to discover that nobody would be there to meet me. When I first came to the U.S. I went through so many situations where I had left a place with no one to see me off, and arrived at my destination only to find myself all alone, with no one to meet me.

"That caused me to wonder if there would be anybody to greet me when that big moment of crossing over comes. So one night I had a dream where my secretary Marlyn told me that you had called me on the phone. Unfortunately I had been away so I didn't get to talk to you.

"I woke up and told Doris about the dream, and she suggested I go into meditation and try to contact you. I did, and was able to make contact. I asked you what it was that you wanted to talk with me about on the phone. You said that the message you had for me was that you would wait for me. Do you recall any such event where you called me on the phone to talk to me?"

"Yes, I do," Asne replied "and I talked to your secretary Marlyn. I left a message with her to tell you that I'd wait for you. But evidently she didn't deliver that message to you. But when you contacted me in meditation, I told you that I would be waiting for you. I wouldn't let you make that transition without being the first one there to welcome you. So don't concern yourself anymore about it."

"It's so comforting to have you say this." I responded. "But tell me, how can I be absolutely sure that you'll meet me when I arrive in heaven? Can you give me some special kind of assurance that you will be waiting for me?"

"I can, and I will. Just wait and see. You won't be disappointed, I assure you. I'll take care of you like I did when the man from planet Htrae took you to another universe, and when Sir Reginald escorted us to the class room. I had arranged it all while I obtained the pass for you."

Asne looked at me with compassionate eyes to let me know that she understood, and would live up to her promise.

"It sure would have been great if I'd been able to visit one of the museums and other pavilions, and listen to many more lectures. How fantastic it would be to visit the Angelic School! You're sure I don't have any time left for these visits?" I wished there was time for all that, and much more. I waited for a favorable reply from my brother and sister.

"Your visitor's pass has expired." Jacob replied, pointing to my badge, which had turned to the color red. "You see," he continued, "when you received your badge it was all white. But as time progressed a red color became visible at the bottom of the badge. Little by little the red covered more and more of it, until now the entire pass is red. That's how I know that your visitor's pass has expired. That's how the people you talked to knew how much time you had left here."

"Well, now I finally understand how all those people knew. And here I thought they were extremely intuitive."

Jacob continued, "When you get back to Earth we encourage you to share with others about this visit."

"Here we are at the last gate before departure." Asne broke in.

We proceeded through the gate. I handed my visitor's pass to an official, who then signed a declaration stating that I was leaving on good terms. The official pointed to a door across the room, indicating that was the way out. Asne and Jacob walked with me.

It was a sad moment for me. I felt like I was in mourning. Leaving this wonderful place didn't seem right. It had been indescribably wonderful to see my sister and brother again, as well as the others I had known. Now it was about to end. Before we went any further, I stopped and took a close look at Asne and Jacob. I loved them very much, and told them so. They assured me of their love with compassionate words and long and tender hugs.

Just as I was ready to open the door I was cautioned to wait a few minutes. The wait was necessary, I was told for the right planet to appear outside the door. Then I opened the door and we stepped outside.

In an instant we were back at the place on the road near the beach where they had first appeared to me. I was still amazed that we could travel so far in just a blink of an eye.

Asne and Jacob had to get back as soon as possible to attend to their assigned classes. Hurriedly we said goodbye, but with enough time for a warm embrace. Before I could say a word they transformed themselves into two bright lights.

Then they vanished.

They disappeared as quickly as when they had earlier appeared to me.

I Looked in the direction I believed they had gone, and squinted, hoping to see them in the far distance. I looked, trying to pierce the clouds, to see far beyond the horizon in hopes of catching another glimpse of them. But there was nothing there, except for some clouds draping the blue sky. I stood there for a while and thought of what had happened to me.

It was unbelievable!

This experience had been far beyond my wildest hopes and expectations. The feeling of being on sacred ground embraced me like a warm and gentle blanket. To me this ground, where Asne and Jacob had stood moments earlier, had become hallowed. I found it difficult to put my feet on it, and therefore didn't dare to walk across it. Making sure that I didn't disturb any of the cherished vibrations surrounding that area, I walked around it.

Except for a soft, calm breeze slowly moving over the ground, it was very still. A hush had fallen, and I experienced again the same unforgettable warm feelings I had when I first stepped into that new and sparkling world with Asne and Jacob. It was as if they had left a touch of Heaven before they said goodbye and vanished.

Slowly I walked toward the beach. That's where it all began. Perhaps they'll be there waiting for me? But inwardly I knew it was only wishful thinking.

I spotted Doris, with Jay and Connie--still looking for colorful stones.

"Who were those people you were talking to?" Doris asked. "For a while I thought I knew them but I wasn't sure. They were too far away. Are they still here?"

"You knew them, all right. Too bad you didn't come over. They were Asne and Jacob."

"But sometime ago you told us that they had been dead for several years." Connie declared. "So why did they appear to you now?"

"It's a long story. I'll tell you all about it over lunch." We walked over to Slocum's restaurant. As we approached it the aroma of grilled fish, roast beef, hamburgers and French fries wafted from the door and with a smile enticed us to enter.

Having been shown a table that overlooked the marina we placed our order with Renee. While waiting for our lunch to be served I didn't waste any time telling them about my experience. And I explained to Doris that Asne and Jacob were not sufficiently advanced to transport more than one person to the first level of Heaven. Perhaps next time, if there might be a a next time, they will be able to transport both of us to Heaven with them.

I told them everything I had seen and heard in as much detail as I possibly could. There was so much to tell, and as I took them through all the wonderful happenings I started to experience them all over again.

As I continued my voice lost its strength from the feeling of awe that came over me. "The places they took me to were literally out of this world. I have heard the most intriguing things, seen some wonderful sights, and met some very inspiring people! I would like to have taken a lot of people along on this journey.

"But all I can do now is just tell you and hopefully many others about it. This has been an amazing and unbelievable journey" I exclaimed in wonderment. As I spoke tears came to my eyes. Again I looked into the far distant horizon hoping that my brother and sister would return again and take us both on another wonderful journey. But nothing like that happened.

The whole experience had been so real. But who, besides Doris, Connie and Jay, would believe me? I thought. On the other hand it didn't really matter. I knew where I had been, and to me it was real. To try to convince others would be useless. Each person had to do his or her own convincing.

Doris broke the silence "You know, this experience is something you must share with others."

"Yes, I know." I replied. "Jacob encouraged me to do just that. But who will believe me?"

"Those with ears to hear, and eyes to see." Doris simply replied.

Renee returned, and said to me,.."There was somebody here looking for you Aron. A very beautiful woman with black hair, pleasant smile, and a man with blond hair and gray eyes. They needed to see you so I invited them to wait, because I expected that you'd come in for lunch. I offered them a cup of coffee and asked if they'd like to have a hamburger while they waited for you. They thanked me, and sat at this same table."

Excitement grew in my heart. It would be delightful to have some kind of confirmation that my journey had been more than a dream. "Do you remember," I asked, "where each of them was sitting?"

"The woman was sitting in the same chair you are, and the man was in the chair where Doris is. But they realized they didn't have time to wait. She asked for a piece of paper and an envelope, wrote a message, slipped it into the envelope, put your name on it and asked me to give it to you. They couldn't have been gone for more than a few minutes. Perhaps you met them out in the parking lot?" She handed me the envelope, and returned to the kitchen.

I eagerly opened it, and read the message.

"Asne and Jacob were really here!" I gasped.

Tears began rolling down my cheeks as I handed the message to Doris. This was the assurance Asne had promised before we parted.

The slip of paper contained only six words:
"I'll be waiting for you. Asne."